GIDEON'S FIRE

He did not really feel afraid. It was as much an impulse and a reflex action as anything which made him cover his face with his bent left arm, and thrust his way into the room. He felt the agonising heat at the back of his hand, felt pain at his forehead and the back of his neck. He tried to see beneath his arm. He glimpsed a child with her nightdress blazing, standing on a bed – a screaming torch. He lowered his head, struggled to take off his tunic and wrap it round the child as she stood there. He felt a crackling sound above, and realised that his hair was burning beneath the rim of his helmet – the child's hair had set his alight. There was agonising pain at his eyes. He staggered to the window. He saw a crowd in the street.
He thought he heard someone cry: "*Jump!*"
He held the child. The window was three stories high, and there were only the people below.
"*Jump!*" they screamed.

Gideon's Fire

John Creasey
as
J. J. Marric

CORONET BOOKS
Hodder Paperbacks Ltd., London

Copyright © 1961 by the Executors of
John Creasey deceased
First published August 1961
by Hodder & Stoughton Ltd.
Coronet edition 1963
Fourth impression 1975

Made and Printed in Great Britain
for Coronet Books,
Hodder Paperbacks Ltd.,
St. Paul's House, Warwick Lane,
London EC4P 4AH
by Cox & Wyman Ltd,
London, Reading and Fakenham

ISBN 0 340 00868 7

CONTENTS

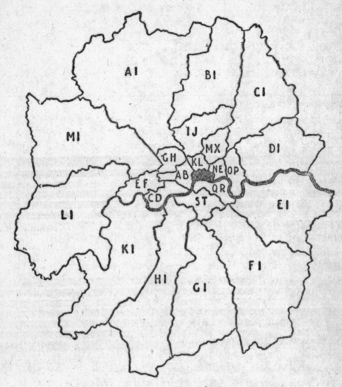

SKETCH MAP OF GIDEON'S TERRITORY

The map conforms only approximately to the boundaries of the
Metropolitan and City Police Forces, and the divisional reference
letters do not coincide with the real London divisional letters or
boundaries

CHAPTER I

THE FIRST FIRE

LONDON lay sleeping.

Here and there a car sped along the grey, deserted streets, the darkness broken by the faint misty light of a sliver of moon, or by the dimmed headlights of the car. The main streets were gilded by the brightness of street lamps, here and there neon colours struck garish against the glow. Over to the west a faint red tinged the sky above Piccadilly Circus, but in the East End only a few lights were on. It was silent, dull, dismal except near the docks, where a white radiance showed the ships being worked to catch the morning tide.

Policemen plodded, a few thieves judged the moments to sidle safely past the law to their snug homes. Most of the night's crimes and most of the night's arrests had been made, the cells of the Divisional police stations had their quotas of men under charge, for being drunk, for being found on enclosed premises, for burglary, theft, hold-up, violence, for the thousand and one offences which made up the police calendar. There had been one brutal murder, of a fourteen-year-old girl, but this was not yet discovered, no one knew that she was dead and not asleep in her narrow bed. The tired prostitutes were home and sleeping, mostly alone; the hotels were like morgues, and any sound seemed loud.

Police Constable Jarvis, of the QR Division, which was south of the Thames and famous in song with its Lambeth Walk and its Old Kent Road, was probably one of the most unremarkable policemen in the Metropolitan Police Force. He was thirty-five, married, with three children nicely staggered at the ages of ten, seven and four, an arrangement controlled, although Jarvis did not realise it, by his busy and competent wife. Jarvis knew Police Regulations off by heart and knew his job inside out, but although he had spent ten years in this Division, one of the toughest in London, he had never once encountered serious trouble, and it did not occur to him even remotely that he might run into any tonight.

He had been called to the bodies of murdered people, but long after the crime had been committed. Street fights outside the pubs on Saturday nights somehow always happened on another man's beat. He had attended his share of accidents and rendered first aid several times, but this was part of the routine of his job. He had made a few arrests, but never of any criminal of note, and he had no desire to improve on this record. He was a satisfied man who took nearly everything for granted, who was 'good' in the sense that he was almost oblivious of temptation. For the first few years of his marriage his wife had worked; soon after their first child Jarvis had won a substantial dividend on the football pools. All this was safely invested, and the interest nearly doubled his wages.

Only twice in his police career had he been compelled to use his truncheon, and only five times had he used his whistle. Yet it never occurred to him to think that life was dull.

He turned out of the Old Kent Road towards a short, narrow street where there were several shops, including a fried fish shop, a newsagent's, a grocer and provision merchant, a television, radio and cycle shop and a shoe repairer. This was a kind of oasis of trade in a drab sea of little houses, with a few old tenement buildings near them, looking rather like the rotted hulks of ships long derelict. There would have been more of these tenement buildings but for the bombing years ago – so long ago in fact that a whole generation had been brought up where bombs had fallen, without the slightest knowledge of the fear that the holocaust could bring. There were great plans, becoming sear and dusty in the Town Hall and in the Ministry of Housing, for a big building project to wipe out all of this slum area and replace it with bright new flats with television aerials built in. These plans had lain fallow for so long that even their creators had almost forgotten to hope for their realisation. The Minister, when reminded, would say with justification that not everything could be done at once.

In this area of slum buildings there lived a few sneak thieves, and twice in the past two weeks one of the shops had been broken into, and a few poundsworth of goods stolen — mostly cigarettes, chocolates and radio spares. This was the kind of petty crime which often came Jarvis's way, and he believed he knew who the burglar was. If he were right, it was an Italian waiter who worked at one of the West End's cheaper night clubs and usually reached home about half past three. It was now three-fifteen, and Jarvis proposed to take up a position from which he could watch the shops when this waiter came home. He had everything worked out, because he knew the waiter's habits thoroughly; he knew the habits of most of the people on his beat because it was his job.

Behind the shops were ten tall tenement buildings, each with five stories, each with outside staircases, each with ten apartments, so each housed ten families. Over five hundred people lived in that tiny area, and most of these were sleeping. The doorway of the one nearest the shops would make an ideal hiding place, and Jarvis plodded over to it, took up his position, glanced at the illuminated dial of his watch and saw that it was twenty minutes past three; he had time for an unhurried drag. He took out a cigarette, cupped a match, lit it without much of the flame showing, drew deeply, and flicked the match away when sure that it was out. The April night was chilly without being cold. The moon had dropped behind the roof of the house opposite. A hum of sound from the docks across the river became more audible, now — and then Jarvis heard the click-click-click of a cycle with a broken spoke, and was sure that his man was approaching.

The cyclist came into sight, his face shown up pale and thin by a street lamp. The machine clicked past, and Jarvis left his hiding place to watch. As he did so, a dark figure appeared from the doorway of one of the other tenement buildings, a few yards away. Jarvis was surprised to see this, but not startled, and his first thought was that this newcomer might be the thief after all. The red glow of the cyclist's rear lamp looked very bright until it was hidden by the man from

the tenement, who turned his back on Jarvis without knowing he was there, and began to walk hurriedly towards the
corner and the shops. Jarvis intended to catch the thief red-
handed, and felt now that he had a double chance of success.
There was no hurry. All he had to do was to watch the
shops after allowing the thief to break in. He drew sur-
reptitiously at his cigarette before nipping it out, and was
not really surprised nor as disappointed as he might have
been when the cyclist passed the shops. The white front and
the red rear lights reflected on the grocery store's windows.
The other man was still on foot, a rather slim, dark figure,
wearing a loose fitting macintosh or raincoat which flapped
a little as he walked; no cloth coat would do that.

This man crossed the road towards the shops.

"Got him," Jarvis murmured aloud, and wondered
whether the thief would force the front door, or go round
the back. He was so sure that he had the man cornered that
he was astounded when he saw him move away from the
newspaper shop, with its valuable stock of cigarettes. He was
now wheeling a bicycle, which had been leaning against
some bill boards. Jarvis remembered that he had seen that
bicycle before without realising that it was there. Had he
actually passed it and given himself time to reflect, he might
have realised that it could mean that the thief was already
at work; he had been so sure of the waiter and the success of
his own straightforward plan. Now, the second man swung
into the saddle of his machine, and began to pedal away.

He had no lights on the machine.

The waiter had gone; this man obviously wasn't going to
burgle a shop here; and Jarvis was thrown off his mental
balance. But he quickly recovered it, for the man on the
bicycle was committing a breach of the law by cycling without lights. Jarvis raised his voice:

"You there! Lights!"

It was a clear, carrying voice, and there was no doubt
that it reached the cyclist, but it did not have the effect
which Jarvis anticipated. The cyclist seemed to crouch
down and put on speed. No lights appeared. The cycle
hummed like a dart towards a corner and swung round as if

the man was on a racing track, not on the narrow south London streets.

"Bloody fool," Jarvis muttered, now really disgruntled, but he did not read any particular significance into what had happened. A lot of people rode without lights, and if this chap's lamps were not in working order he would be anxious to get as far away as possible so that he couldn't be stopped. Jarvis now began to speculate on his identity. He had come out of Number 17 – the third remaining tenement building, the middle one of the five in this battered terrace. Standing on the kerb and looking at the now deserted street, Jarvis began to go systematically through the people who lived there. The fourth floor left flat was empty – the new people were due to move in next week. Certain families could be ruled out, certain men lodgers, too, for only three men who lived in that apartment had the same kind of figure as the man who had hurried away.

"I'll get him one of these days," Jarvis boasted to the quiet night. "I wouldn't mind betting it was Miller. Can't think why he'd be going out at half past three, though. Could have had a quarrel with his missus, I suppose." Miller was a man in the middle twenties who had married a woman fifteen years his senior, for her money. There were two children by her first marriage and three, all under five, of this marriage; it was well known that they lived like cat and dog. "Miller isn't up to anything, is he?" Jarvis asked the silent street. "If she's keeping him short again, he might —"

Jarvis broke off, and sniffed.

London smog and London smoke did little to help any native's sense of smell, but there was no mistaking the stench of burning which came from the stairway behind him – the stairway from which the thin man had come. Jarvis turned towards it. He knew the tenement buildings inside out. The staircase had one flight to each floor in the open air, one flight to each floor under cover. There were front doors on either side at street level and at each landing level. When he reached the first landing, the stench was even stronger, and in and out of the beam of his torch crept wisps of smoke.

"Dunno that I like this," said Jarvis to himself, and sprinted up another flight of stairs. As he turned the corner, the bright beam caught a swirling grey patch, and there was no longer any doubt that this was a fire which had got a quick hold. He took out his whistle, and blew a long, ear-splitting blast which screeched up and down the narrow staircase. Then he tucked the whistle away, and bellowed: *"Fire!* Show a leg – *fire* !" As he shouted, he ran up to the next landing, and saw thick smoke above it; the fire seemed to be coming from the fourth floor, and he thought that he could hear the crackling of flames. He grabbed the iron knocker of the door nearest him, thundered on it, and kept shouting: *"Fire!"* until he pulled out his handkerchief and held it in front of his face as he charged up the next flight of stairs.

It did not occur to him that he was being brave.

He reached the landing, and saw the red glow beneath the door of Apartment 8 – the Millers' apartment, with Miller's wife and five kids in it. He hesitated for an agonising moment, trying to recall exactly what the book said, remembering that he must do nothing to create too much of a draught.

"To hell with a draught," he muttered. "If I don't get that door down they'll burn to a cinder." He drew back and flung himself at the door, his right shoulder towards it. The door sagged. He saw a scared-looking man above him, the elderly tenant of one of the higher flats. "Get everyone out of there," Jarvis ordered wheezily and began to choke as the smoke caught his breath. He was not worried about the people above or below, they could get out; but the Miller family would have had it if they didn't get out quick. He shouldered the door again, felt it give, but knew it might be a long time before he could get it down. A man in stark white pyjamas came hurrying up the stairs towards him, a woman in a billowing nightdress gaping at the bosom, was standing below.

"Send for the fire service," Jarvis called. "Then get a ladder up to the Millers' window."

"Okay !" The man spun round. "Look out, Elsie !" he

shouted, and sounded more excited than Jarvis, who drew back with massive deliberation, and flung all his weight at the door.

It gave way.

A roar of flame and a blast of oven-hot air swept out at him, and nearly choked him. He thought he heard a scream. He saw flames filling a small passage, saw the door of one room in a red-hot, blistering mass. The roaring died away now that the draught had slackened, and he heard the screaming of a child inside the room.

He did not really feel afraid. It was as much an impulse and a reflex action as anything which made him cover his face with his bent left arm, and thrust his way into the room. He felt the agonising heat at the back of his hand, felt pain at his forehead and the back of his neck. He tried to see beneath his arm. He glimpsed a child with her night-dress blazing, standing on a bed – a screaming torch. He felt a floor board crack beneath him. He lowered his head, struggled to take off his tunic and wrap it round the child as she stood there, but he felt a sickening sense of hopelessness, despair and fear. He felt a crackling sound above, and realised that his hair was burning beneath the rim of his helmet – the child's hair had set his alight. There was agonising pain at his eyes. There was the roaring of the fire, the fury of crackling, the groaning boards; only the screaming had stopped. He staggered towards the window, preparing to break it with his elbow. He hugged the child tightly to him with one hand and bent his elbow and cracked it against the big pane. As the glass shattered, he heard the ringing of a fire-engine bell. He saw a crowd in the street. He thought he heard someone cry: *"Jump!"* He still held the child. This window was three stories high, and there were only the people below, some of them holding a blanket.

"Jump !" they screamed.

He lifted the silent child up and down in his arms, not knowing whether she was dead or alive. He could not call down to the people, for his tongue seemed paralysed, but the silence which suddenly fell upon them told him that they knew what he held.

He tossed the child out, saw her fall, saw her caught in the blanket. His head was swimming. *His head was burning.* His trousers, his shirt, his shoes were on fire. The noise of the fire-engine grew louder, but he did not see it swing into the street. He felt darkness coming over him, tinged with red, he felt himself swaying backwards and knew that he was losing consciousness. Then he realised that someone else was here with him: a man. In his last fading moment of consciousness he realised that it was Miller, wrapped in a burning coat, hugging another blazing torch, another child.

Then Police Constable Jarvis collapsed.

CHAPTER II

GIDEON HEARS

GEORGE GIDEON, the Commander of the Criminal Investigation Department at New Scotland Yard, gave his wife a rather perfunctory kiss the morning after the fire, said: "I'll try not to be late, Kate," and went off only vaguely aware that she was standing at the porch of their house in Hurlingham, smiling until he was out of sight. At the last moment he turned and waved again, thought warmly about her for as long as it took him to reach the corner, and then forgot her. It was not that he was preoccupied with any particular official problem; he was simply aware that he would be half an hour late at the office. No one, least of all the Assistant Commissioner for Crime, would raise an eyebrow if the executive chief of the Department was hours late, but to Gideon punctuality was both virtue and obligation. If he turned up later than he had promised to, then he could hardly blame his men for slacking. Joe Bell, now his chief *aide*, would not slack consciously, but lesser men probably would. In an almost exasperating way the Department had come to depend too much on its Commander, and any slackness which began at the top could spread down the ranks and even out into the Divisions. Inevitably several superintendents, including two seniors, would want to see him this morning, mostly on cases needing urgent attention. If he kept them kicking their heels, it would take the edge off their keenness and might lead to the failure of a case or the loss of a wanted man.

Gideon, although he would have scoffed had anyone suggested it, was at once a slave and a martyr to his job.

Both he and Kate had overslept, and the children had all got themselves off, to work or to school, thinking it a kindly gesture not to disturb their parents. So it had been, but he wished that they hadn't misplaced their kindness this morning. He had bolted breakfast, with Kate protesting that a few minutes really couldn't make any difference, and when he reached the door of the garage he was trying to persuade himself that she was quite right, and it was absurd to behave as if every minute mattered. He ought to take things more easily, and get rid of a responsibility complex.

The thought made him grin.

"What a hope," he said, and unlocked the padlock and pushed up the door which worked on a roller and slid beneath the roof. His car, a not very new Humber Hawk, black and shining, almost filled the small garage. He had to squeeze into the driving seat and then back out with great care. As he turned on the ignition, a green truck appeared in his driving mirror, and instead of passing, it stopped. "Damned fool," said Gideon to himself, and started the engine; at least that gave no trouble. He tooted his horn, and the sound was deafening in here, but it did not make the truck move on. If he squeezed out so as to complain he might find himself watching the tail of the truck; the best thing was to be patient, but after a few minutes he began to play an exasperated tune on the horn.

The truck moved at last. Gideon backed out, and was half-way into the road when a horn screeched at him, and he jammed on his brakes. A Jaguar flashed by in the mirror, going much too fast.

"This is my morning," Gideon said aloud, and without thinking about it, he took himself in hand. Every movement, of foot, hand and eye, became more considered. He swung slowly into the road, pulled up, and was about to get out to close the garage when Kate appeared, her fine tall body moving with careless ease, as if she were breasting life with an abiding if latent passion. She drew up to the window, and said:

"I'll close the garage, dear."

"Bless you," Gideon said. "Any message?"

"No, I just came to see why you were so long." Kate stood back. "Have a good day," she added, and waved and turned to the garage.

Gideon drove a little more slowly than usual, because of his deep-set belief that no man in a car should ever be in a hurry – except occasionally Flying Squad cars – but by the time he was moving along New Kings Road, Fulham, past the Eelbrook Common and towards Chelsea and West-minster, he had forgotten all that, and was cutting along at ten miles an hour over the official thirty. Traffic began to build up, but did not irritate him; Kate had driven irritation away, which was Kate's great gift. Gideon thought back to last night, a golden night, and the reason for oversleeping. He chuckled, then nipped past a van which looked top heavy with sacks of onions and carrots.

He began to think of the different cases which the men waiting for him would want to discuss. There was Riddell, newly appointed a superintendent, on his first big murder investigation, the case of the three young women found buried in the same grave near Chichester. Riddell had been away on the job for a week, and had telephoned last night to say that he thought he ought to have a talk with Gideon; that meant he was out of his depth. Cornish would want guidance on last week's bank robbery, when three thieves had got away with twenty-seven thousand pounds after tunnelling beneath two rows of shops and a main road; one of the men had been caught but the others and the money were still missing. Lemaitre, once his chief assistant and now a kind of general factotum at the Yard, sometimes on night duty, sometimes on day, *locum tenens* for any senior official on sick leave or holiday leave, was bursting at the

seams to make an arrest in a share-pushing case, but Gideon
wasn't too certain that the time was ripe. There were a
dozen other, lesser cases, and there would be new ones both
for the Yard and for the Divisions. He had an appointment
with the Assistant Commissioner for noon, and would have
his work cut out to get everything else arranged and all the
men briefed in time to keep the appointment. Before the
day was done he was going to rue the loss of that half-hour,
but he was now quite good-tempered about the prospect.

He turned into the Yard, found his usual parking space
blocked by a car he didn't recognise, left his key with a constable who came hurrying to help, and went up the flight of
stone steps. It was on this daily morning walk that Gideon
really seemed to become part of the big red-brick buildings.
He was a tall man, six feet two, massive, with a thick chest,
slightly rounded shoulders smoothly fitted with an excel-
lently tailored coat, and unexpectedly flat at the stomach.
His jowl sometimes looked rather fleshy and there was a hint
of overweight at the back of his neck, but his belly was as
hard as a board, and he took pride in his physical strength.
That strength gave Gideon much of his quality, for it explained his complete confidence in himself. Sight of him
mounting the steps, head jutting forward, taking in everything he saw, was an indication of his character: the way he
always bored ahead, without allowing anything to push him
off the path he wanted to go, his weighty, sometimes slow
movements sometimes giving an indication of remorseless-
ness; where he meant to go, George Gideon would go.

He walked along the passage which connected the new
and the old buildings, well aware that by now the telephone
in his office had rung and been answered, that Bell and
possibly Lemaitre would be in the office with the morning's
reports ready, that everyone waiting to see him would know
that he was on the way, some of them on edge in case he
found fault with work done or proposals made.

He heard the click of his own door closing as he reached
the passage leading to it, and marvelled that grown men like
Lemaitre and Bell – Bell was in his early sixties – should
behave rather like schoolboys wondering if the head was on

the prowl; but it did no harm. Other doors were ajar, men were glancing at him, he saw brown-clad Riddell standing by a desk, obviously impatient; Riddell, who had once been the slackest man in the Department, was now always on the go. Gideon pretended not to notice him, and thrust open the door of his own office. Lemaitre, a tall, thin, almost weedy man, with a bony face, bright and very alert grey eyes, with his brown hair cropped close almost in a crew cut, his bow tie a little too bright in green and blues, his grey suit somehow contriving to look a little loud, turned round from the window where he was looking down at the river. Joe Bell was sitting at his pedestal desk, a small one in a corner opposite Gideon's big one. Joe was a shorter man, and rather plump. His thin fluffy hair was grey, he looked all of his sixty-odd years, and he had a kind of benignity which Gideon found restful. Nothing ever made Bell panic, and no one knew more about the Yard or the ways of the police, criminals and the judiciary. Bell might have gone a long way had he had a little of Gideon's drive or his fire; but as it was, his tweeds always wanted pressing, he was never really closely shaved, his pipe always wanted scraping.

"'Morning, Gee-Gee," Lemaitre greeted, with the privilege of long friendship and familiarity. "You broken a leg or something?"

"I swam here," Gideon said, nodding to Joe Bell. "Didn't you see me while you were counting the windows in County Hall?"

"Shurrup," retorted Lemaitre. His voice had a Cockney twang, and he always spoke as if he were in a hurry to get this subject finished and the next one on the way. "There's Riddell sweating on the top line because he ought to be on the way down to Chichester, there's Cornish —"

"We'll get round to it all, Lem," Gideon said, and took off his coat, draping it over the back of the leather-seated chair behind his big, old-fashioned desk. He sat down. "Anything much in, Joe?"

"'Fraid so," said Bell, quietly.

"Hmp. What?" Gideon looked sharply across the desk, aware of but ignoring Lemaitre's impatience, knowing that

Bell would not speak like that unless this had been a bad night. Whenever London had a heavy night of crime, Gideon felt a kind of personal responsibility, for it should be the work of the police to stop crime as well as to make sure it was punished. He was not only part of his job, he was part of London.

"Fourteen-year-old girl strangled in her bed over at Islington," Bell answered.

"Sex job?"

"Couldn't be nastier. Hands tied to the bed-posts, and raped."

"Oh, God." Gideon felt momentarily sick, and thought, as he always did when a girl had been the victim of some crime, of his own daughters, Prudence, Priscilla and Penelope. Three faces, bright and eager, seemed to loom in front of him – three pairs of eyes were questioning him. *Why?*

"What line have we got?" asked Gideon.

"Not much," answered Bell. "Carson of KL was on the blower only ten minutes ago, wanted a word with you."

"Get him on the line, will you?"

"Yes."

"George," intervened Lemaitre, "I know you're going to have a thick morning, how about letting me get cracking? You know as well as I do that we've got enough to charge Ericson with. He floated those shares at a pound each and three parts of the prospectus was a lie. We —"

"Have we got him tight enough to be sure of a conviction?" Gideon asked.

"*I* think so."

"Anything more in about the case?"

"No, but —"

"Tell you what," said Gideon, as if struck with a new idea, "you go and see if you can find Roscoe. If we can get Roscoe to give evidence, we'll have Ericson tight as a drum. What about it?"

"You know damned well that Roscoe's crossed the channel!"

"Not sure that he has, Lem," Gideon said. "I think he

tried to make us think he had, but that's all. Have another go."

"But dammit —"

A telephone bell rang. "This'll be Carson," said Bell, and Gideon picked up one of three telephones on his desk and said into it: "Gideon." He covered the mouthpiece with his big left hand, grinned at Lemaitre, and whispered: "It won't work, Lem, just because I've got a lot to do this morning you needn't think you're going to rush me into picking Ericson up. We can't do that until we've got more evidence, and the quickest way to evidence will be Roscoe. Why don't you see if that thing you call a mind can work? . . . Hallo, yes, who . . . Oh, hallo, Carson." He waved Lemaitre away, ignoring the other's wry grimace and exaggerated groan. Both Lemaitre and Bell knew that Gideon had put the fraud case out of his mind, and was now giving his whole attention to Carson of KL Division. He began to frown, for Carson was one of the rule-of-thumb men, very efficient of his kind but almost entirely dispassionate. He could go into clinical details as to what had happened to the fourteen-year-old Ivy Manson at her home in Islington.

Lemaitre said: "Like a brick wall, that's what Gee-Gee is," and went out. He closed the door softly.

". . . so there isn't any definite line," Carson was saying. "There are four flats in the house, all self-contained. Any one of the tenants could have got in, the Mansons are still about fifty years behind the times, Commander. They leave a key dangling inside the front door, so all you have to do to get it is open the letter box and hook it out by the string. No doubt the key was used —"

"That key?" demanded Gideon.

"I didn't mean that one, I meant *a* key. No scratches on the door, none on the window, only possible way the beast could have got in was by the door, using a key."

"Do you want any help?" Gideon asked.

"That's really what I wanted to talk to you about, Commander." Carson was formal. "I think that everyone in the street should be questioned, and that will need more men than I can put on the job unless I am to neglect other investigations. I would like at least six additional men."

"I'll fix it."

"Thank you. Bell has sent a fingerprints officer over, and my murder team is on the spot in strength," Carson went on. "So far, there is nothing to go on and the first essential is to find out whether anyone was seen coming into the house during the night. I am inclined to think that the murderer knows the family, the indications are that he opened the front door and went straight to the girl's bedroom, which is a small one leading off the kitchen, which lies between it and the rest of the flat – it's almost cut off, in fact. It is evident that he gagged her before she could call out for help, and . . ."

"Check the whole neighbourhood for schizos and anyone known to the police for the slightest sex abnormality – indecent behaviour, indecent assault, you know the drill," Gideon said. "This is one we want finished in a hurry, we don't want that brute wandering about loose."

"I couldn't agree more," said Carson. "Thank you, Commander." His manner told Gideon that he was annoyed because he had been reminded of the obvious, but once he put the receiver down, Gideon forgot about Carson and the child; he had to concentrate on whatever Bell had next.

"Next," he invited.

"Only one other bad one," Bell said. "It's the top one on your desk." In front of Gideon were all the files on all the cases going through the Yard, as well as a complete list of all the major crimes reported during the night. "Fire, out in Lambeth," Bell went on. "One of those old tenement buildings. Whole family was wiped out – mother, five kids, and the father. Several other people burned and suffering from shock, and the whole building was gutted – place went up like a match-box." Bell paused, and Gideon sat still, knowing that the worst was still to come; and Bell looked older even than his years as he went on: "One of our chaps looks like being the eighth victim. The last I heard he hadn't much chance. Uniformed man named Jarvis, one for the

George Medal according to the reports. But the worst of it is, George, it was arson. Started with petrol. No doubt about it."

CHAPTER III

DYING MAN

GIDEON read the report from Superintendent Manning, of QR Division, still oblivious of the men waiting to see him, even Riddell and his sense of urgency, and of the girl at Islington. That had been hideous; in its way, this was worse. Manning was not only a sound Divisional head, he put in thorough if wordy reports, and still liked to do them in his own handwriting – not copper plate, but very small and legible. Manning had been told of the fire at half past four that morning, and gone over to see for himself; that was characteristic, for he was extremely conscientious. More-over, he had co-ordinated reports from his own men, from the Chief Fire Officer of the district, and statements from neighbours. There was no doubt about the arson, and the gallon can in which the petrol had been kept had been found among the charred wreckage, burnt almost out of recognition, but with the tell-tale sediment or ash that petrol always left after this kind of burning. Petrol had been thrown about the flat, as far as the first indications went, one suggestion was that a man had stood at the front door, poured the petrol out along the passage hallway off which all the rooms led, and then set light to it and closed the door. In all the tenement buildings there was a gap between the bottom of the door and the floor, and petrol had undoubtedly flowed into the rooms where the members of the family had been sleeping. Fumes appeared to have overcome the mother and the two elder children, who slept in the same room, and the remains of their bodies had been found in their beds. One, very young, child had been found in a cot in the other bed-

room. Two had been thrown out of the window, one by the
constable, Jarvis, the other by the father of the children,
George Miller. Miller and Jarvis had jumped, but Miller
had died on his way to hospital, where the two children had
been dead on arrival.

Gideon felt his heart savaged by what he had to read.

The report went on:

"Police Constable Jarvis was still alive when he arrived
at the Lambeth Hospital, and at eight forty-five remained
alive, but the hospital authorities hold out little hope of his
recovery. There is a faint possibility that he will recover
consciousness enough to make a statement, and two men are
at his bedside to make sure that nothing is missed. His wife,
Emily Maude, is also at his side. Their three children, a boy
aged four, and girls aged seven and ten, are being cared for
by neighbours, and the Division will make sure that everything necessary is done for them and for Mrs. Jarvis. Jarvis
is reported to be suffering from first degree burns over a
large area of his body, and it is clear that these burns were
incurred during his attempt to rescue the family.

"The flat immediately above the one where the Miller
family lived has been empty for two weeks, so no one was
burnt there. Tenants of all the other flats in the building
had time to escape.

"One person, an elderly woman named Forsyth, who
lives in a small house opposite the tenement buildings has so
far made a statement which may give some assistance. She
suffers from insomnia, got out of bed in her front bed-sitting
room, and made tea during the early hours of the morning.
She reports that she cannot be positive of the actual time,
but she noticed certain events in the following sequence:

"1. P.C. Jarvis arrive, on foot, and take up a position in
the tenement doorway, apparently as a point of observation.

"2. Jarvis light a pipe or cigarette—she believes a cigarette.

"3. A cyclist pass between her and Jarvis, a man whose
name she does not know but who often passes the house at
about half past three at night.

"4. A man appear from the doorway of the tenement,

two doors removed from Jarvis's point of vantage. This man walked towards the shops.

"5. Jarvis followed this man and called out to him after the man mounted a bicycle. The only word that the woman heard clearly was *lights* – from which it may be inferred that a cyclist was riding off without lights on his machine.

"Following further close questioning of this witness," the report went on, "we are using all endeavours to find out the identity of the two men. The first cyclist she saw and who passes along Gill Street every morning, appears to be the most likely source of information."

Gideon finished reading, looked up, and saw that Bell was glancing through some other reports, but obviously with only half of his attention, for he also looked up.

"That's the second ugly customer we want badly," he said. "Funny thing how often these bad shows come in pairs."

"Yes," agreed Gideon, and nodded. "Lot of things we want on this one. Identity of each man – how did petrol get into the apartment – anyone hate the Millers?" He drew in a hiss of breath. "Could anyone hate a family enough to want to wipe them all out? Doesn't make much sense, but there was the Manuel case. We need the motive, we need . . ." He talked as he made notes on a desk pad, and at the same time reminded himself that this was Manning's job, and that as a uniformed officer from the QR Division was dead or dying, the whole of that Division would be on its toes; there was no need to push Manning yet. He, Gideon, simply wanted to jot down the questions which occurred to him while the news was fresh in his mind; if there was any delay in catching the man who had started the fire, he could go over his notes with Manning.

A telephone rang on his desk; another, on Bell's. Each man lifted a receiver in a single swift, mechanical motion. Gideon heard Bell say: "Soon," and ring off, and then the operator said: "Can you speak to Mr. Manning of QR Division, sir?"

"Put him through."

"Yes, sir . . ."

"Hallo, George," said Manning, in a rather high-pitched voice which sounded slightly affected. "I thought you'd like to know we've found that cyclist. A Soho waiter, named Callini, Guiseppe Callini. He's on his way to the station."

"Might help," said Gideon. "Anything more about Jarvis?"

"Yes," answered Manning, and his voice seemed almost a falsetto. "He passed away, twenty minutes ago. I'm just going to see his widow. George, read my report like Hawk-eye, won't you? There's no one like you for seeing points that others miss and I want to catch this bastard in a hurry."

"I'll try not to miss anything," Gideon promised.

He rang off, made one or two more notes, studied the first page of the report, then put it away from him, glanced at Bell and asked: "Was that Riddell?"

"Yes. Steaming."

"Let's have him in first," said Gideon, and Bell pressed a buzzer. Almost immediately the door opened, and Riddell stalked in. He was tall, well built, a little on the big side, immaculate in a smooth-textured brown suit, with sleekly brushed brown hair, highly polished brown shoes, a business executive of a man. There was a haughty expression in his face, too, a face which somehow missed being handsome although all the features were good. Obviously he found it difficult not to protest that he had been waiting for so long.

"Sorry, Rid, we've got two bad ones in this morning," said Gideon quickly. "And that chap Jarvis died." He took it for granted that Riddell knew what he was talking about, and Riddell openly thawed at this friendly approach. "Take a pew. I've been thinking about your three corpses in the same home-made grave. Think you've got a mass mur-derer?"

"Could be," said Riddell, sitting down. "As a matter of fact, I think I may be on to the chap. The two bodies at the bottom of the grave haven't been identified yet, but Sibley says they're about the same age, late twenties, and one probably died a year before the other. I've had him on the phone. The top one's the same kind of age, but she's only been dead about three weeks. We've traced her. Girl named

Florence Denny, had a little flat of her own in Brighton, secretary to an accountant. He got a telephone message a month ago, saying she was going to move to London because her parents were getting old and she had to look after them. Chap thought it a bit queer, but she was a flighty piece, always out late at nights and seldom early in the morning, so he was glad to let her go. Didn't ask about her, just sent her insurance cards and a week's wages to her flat – generous enough in the circumstances."

Gideon nodded; but although he was looking at Riddell as if concentrating on every word, in fact he kept seeing the report from Manning, and picturing the burning torches of children; from there it was only a step in memory to the girl at Islington. Gagged, assaulted, strangled. Why strangle her? He must make a note to find out if there had been a light in the bedroom, or even one shining from outside, anything which would suggest that the child might have seen her assailant clearly enough to be able to describe or to recognise him. If there had been no light, why had the man strangled her? The gagging to keep her quiet, yes. The rape, yes. But to strangle her – why? It could be a case of sex perversion, or —

He made a surreptitious note on his pad. *'Light.'*

". . . and this chap Harrison, George Harrison, spent a lot of time with her, at dances, pictures, all the fun of Brighton Beach," Riddell was saying. "Married man, wife's a bit of a drip, two children. And this Florence Denny was in the family way. The local police have had Harrison checked under suspicion of receiving, he's clear on that but they've got a pretty full dossier on him. Saved me a lot of trouble. On the strength of what we know, I think we ought to bring Harrison in. It looks as if he gets tired of the girls, takes 'em to a nice quiet spot for the usual, and strangles 'em, with the grave nice and handy. The thing I can't make up my mind about is, should we bring him in and try to make him talk, or would it be better to wait until we can identify the other two women, and prove that he knew them, too? If he did, the case is cut and dried. If he didn't —"

"What do you want to do?" asked Gideon.

"I'd like to have a go at Harrison. I think he would break down."

"Hmm," Gideon said. "See what you mean." Here was a clear case of a Yard man over-anxious to make sure that if anyone made a mistake, it was Gideon. Riddell wanted approval of a course of action simply as a measure of self-defence, whereas Lemaitre was bursting to catch his man. "Rid, if I were you I'd work on the identification of the other two bodies. It may take a few days longer, even a few weeks, but this Harrison is living happily enough with his wife, I take it?"

"Outwardly, yes."

"Has he got any other girl friends?"

"There's a girl he's just started going about with – a Chloe Duval. Can't understand the set-up at all really. His wife doesn't seem to care what he gets up to, provided he keeps her and the children in comfort. He's a motor car salesman, and does pretty well out of it. Nice house at Rottingdean, and" – Riddell saw Gideon glance down at the reports on his desk, and went on rather more hastily – "I know you're busy, but I don't want to go wrong on this case, Commander. I'm having Harrison watched, and if there looks like any funny business with this new girl he's tagging along with, we'll be on to him. The identification of the others could take weeks."

"Why don't you give it another week, and see what the position is then," suggested Gideon. "That will give you and the Sussex chaps time to dig pretty closely into Florence Denny's association with Harrison. Give you time to check back on Harrison's life and girl friends, too – if you can find that a couple of them disappeared about the time these women were killed, then you might get your angle that way. Give it a week," he repeated.

"Very well," said Riddell, obviously not too pleased with the decision. "You won't mind if I get cracking right away?"

"You get moving," urged Gideon. "All we've got to do is

make sure he doesn't get this new fancy of his out in that quiet spot. If he killed the others near there and got away with it, he'll use the same place again."

"I'll watch it," Riddell said, and went out; he let the door close behind him on its softly hissing hinges.

Almost as it closed, a telephone rang on Gideon's desk, and with the usual mechanical movement, he lifted it. "Gideon," he said, and amplified the noted word 'light' with a few scribbled words. "Who? . . . Yes, put him through." He mouthed to Bell: "Get this one." Bell lifted his extension telephone, and Gideon said: "Hallo, Mr. Carmichael, how are you these days?"

Carmichael was the Chief Officer of the London Fire Service, an elderly man not far off the retiring age, who probably knew more about fire, its causes and effects, than any man alive, certainly more than any man in London. His senior assistants liaised with the Yard whenever arson was suspected; the fact that Carmichael had called in person suggested that he had something serious to say.

Carmichael said: "Very well, Mr. Gideon, thank you. Can you spare me half an hour this morning?"

It was a hell of a morning to be faced with that request, and Gideon knew that he ought to say 'no', and make it this afternoon, but the mental picture of those burning children was vivid in his mind, and he said:

"Yes, of course. Half past twelve would suit me best, but —"

"Why don't we have lunch together?" suggested Carmichael. "I have to be at the Home Office at half past eleven. Supposing we meet at your office at half past twelve."

"Right," said Gideon. "Suits me fine."

"I want to talk to you about last night's Lambeth fire," went on Carmichael. "There are one or two features about it and other fires which puzzle me. This will be quite unofficial for the time being, of course."

"Of course," said Gideon, very glad that he had made no difficulties. "Right you are, then. Twelve thirty, here." He rang off, and Bell put down his receiver and settled back in his chair, waiting for Gideon to make some comment. "Any idea what he might have in mind, Joe?"

"No," answered Bell.

"Well, get someone to go over to QR right away, will you, to dig as deep as he can. Ask Manning to be at the end of a telephone at twelve thirty, so that he can bring me right up to date. Don't want Carmichael to think we're slipping. Make sure Carson's on the lookout for someone who knew Ivy Manson, and might have been recognised by her." He paused. "What do you think of Riddell?"

"Came up last night so that he could spend a night at home, his wife still needles him if he's away too much," said Bell. "He wanted to pass the buck, too. You're going to find it pretty tight, aren't you? The Old Man at twelve o'clock, then Carmichael, and it's nearly eleven already."

"You fix the QR job," Gideon ordered, and lifted a receiver. "Ask Mr. Cornish to come in, will you?"

There followed one of the periods which never failed to impress Joe Bell, although he had worked at the Yard for forty years and with Gideon, on and off, for twenty. Gideon in a hurry was an experience in itself. The most fascinating aspect was that although he obviously geared himself up to high speed action, he was able to approach every new subject with calm deliberation, as if warning himself that more haste really did mean less speed. He did not waste a minute and did not let any of the others, from superintendents down to detective inspectors, waste a second. Now and again he refreshed his memory of a case by looking at the reports in front of him, but whether he did that or not, he always seemed to be as familiar with the circumstances of a case as the man who was in direct charge of it. There was Cornish with his inquiry into the bank tunnelling job; Gideon remembered exactly who had been questioned, what tools had been used, how many hours must have been involved. Cornish had failed to trace the two missing men and the money.

"Been thinking about that," Gideon remarked, "and I've

got a feeling that it might be connected with the Bournemouth job two years ago. You were down there, weren't
you?"

"Yes," said Cornish, a heavily built, solid, stolid man,
"but I don't see the connection. That wasn't a tunnelling
job, they broke through a reinforced concrete wall."

"Didn't you say that in this job there were no fingerprints
but a print of a little tear in a glove showed up."

"So what?"

"Same at Bournemouth, surely."

"Blimey, I didn't think of that," said Cornish lugubriously. "Teased us, that print did. Ta. I'll get out the old
photographs and check, George."

He hurried out.

There was an embezzlement job, a few minutes with a
man who was probing into the newest vice racket in the West
End, as long over a smuggling ring suspected of bringing
thousands of watches in from Switzerland, three cases of
missing persons, one case of a stolen lorry load of cigarettes,
three cases which were going through the courts, two of
them at the Old Bailey, a case of the ill-treatment of children
by a foster-mother, two cases of illegal abortion each resulting in a woman's death, one of a diamond robbery from a
Hatton Garden merchant on the boat from Harwich to the
Hook of Holland – and with each of these Gideon dealt
unhurriedly, and yet in the minimum of time. When he
had finished, it was ten minutes to twelve.

"After that lot you deserve a cuppa," Bell declared.

"Forget it," said Gideon. "Ring the A.C.'s secretary and
say I'm on the way. It won't do Rogerson any harm to see
me early." He stood up, pulled the knot of his tie straight,
slipped into his coat, and smoothed down his wiry, iron grey
hair.

Bell said: "I don't know how you do it, George, but you
look as if you've had a morning's rest."

"All went pretty smoothly, didn't it?" asked Gideon.
"Don't forget to check with Manning, and get me a report
on the fire so that I can read it before I see Carmichael. Oh,
and fix a table at the pub across —"

"Carmichael's secretary rang, and says you're to lunch at his club, in Whitehall Place," Bell said. "I said it would suit you."

"It suits me fine," Gideon agreed, and went out, head thrust forward, big body moving in that deliberate and stubbornly aggressive way he had, face expressionless, well aware of the eyes at the doors, the whisper of: "Gee-Gee's on the prowl," the general air of being on their toes. That was a good thing. They were a good lot of men. They had a hell of a lot to do. And today they had started two hunts which every man at the Yard and at the Divisions would slave over.

Little Ivy Manson.

And the seven dead Millers and P.C. Jarvis.

The session with the Assistant Commissioner was about administrative matters, and at a quarter past twelve Gideon went to the cloakroom, washed and brushed up, and hurried along to his office. Bell had the wanted fire report ready. The only additional item was about the waiter, Guiseppe Callini, who said that he could tell the police only one thing: as he had cycled home, another cyclist had passed him at high speed, going towards the docks.

"Pity there's not a bit more," Gideon said, and glanced at the front page headlines of the London evening newspapers on his desk. Each one featured the Lambeth fire, one hinted at sabotage, all had pictures, and across the top of the *Evening Globe* were six photographs in all – of Miller, his wife, and the smiling children of their marriage.

Smiling, happy children.

The story about little Ivy Manson was on an inside page. Gideon glanced at it, and then went out, knowing that Carmichael would be punctual, wondering what the Chief Fire Officer had in mind.

Carmichael held the *Evening Globe* in his right hand, and Gideon judged from the expression on his rather pale, austere face that he felt a deep hatred for this firebug. It was on that instant, as Carmichael turned pale grey eyes towards him, that Gideon sensed what the other man had in mind;

that this might have been one of several such fires and there
might be others to come.

"Seen this?" asked Carmichael, and thrust the newspaper
out.

MEN IN FEAR

"WHAT a terrible thing," said little Mrs. Tennison to her
boarder. "Just think, *eight* people burned to death,
it makes you feel awful, doesn't it?" She was an untidy wisp
of a woman with thin grey hair, thin and rather pointed
features, many lines at her eyes, many bristly grey hairs
sprouting at her chin. Her chest was as flat as a board, and
some people found it almost impossible to believe that the
photograph over the sideboard in the front room was really
of her family; there were four girls and three boys. Mrs.
Tennison would boast in a confidential whisper: "Every one
of them breast fed up to eighteen months, as I stand here. I
never could abide these stodgy new-fashioned foods, what
with giving the poor little things wind *and* constipation . . ."

The second remarkable thing about her was that she had
been widowed for nearly twenty years, and that all of her
carefully nurtured children were married or living abroad.
Dotted about the mantelpiece were pictures of a bewildering
number of grandchildren, all apparently taken at the same
age, all plump and goo-goo eyed. It was like a child photo-
grapher's shop.

For years, Mrs. Tennison had lived by cheerfully accepting
a weekly gift of five pounds from a common pool created by
her family, by taking in boarders, and by shrewd picking of
winners for modest sums. Just now, she had only one
boarder – Mr. Brown. The moment she had set eyes upon
Mr. Brown, she had felt sorry for him. He was such a timid,
frightened little man, with a lost and forlorn look. She did

not know a great deal about him, but he had told her that he had lost his wife and child in an accident, not long ago, and that he was 'picking up the pieces'. In her spontaneus way, Mrs. Tennison's heart went out to Mr. Brown, and she could have made very little profit out of the five guineas a week he paid for board and lodging. Meat twice a day was the rule, although when she had first coped with her family, fresh meat once a week had been the average.

Brown had such worried grey eyes. He had such bloodless, helpless looking lips. He moved so quietly. He spent so much time alone in his room, listening to music on gramophone records of a kind which Mrs. Tennison could neither understand nor appreciate although, undoubtedly, it was 'good' music. She did not know what his main work was, but apparently he took on all kinds of odd jobs. Sometimes he would work by day, sometimes by night. His clothes were of good quality, his two suitcases and one trunk were of good quality, too, there was something of the gentleman about him, which discouraged too many questions. She felt that she was very fortunate to have such a well-mannered gentleman in the house, and hoped that he would stay for a long time. Certainly he had settled in very well.

He had been out at work the previous night, had arrived home about four o'clock, and gone straight to bed. She had heard him, of course; decades of listening to the children coming home at different hours had created a habit of catnapping which the years had not broken. Now, instead of counting them one by one until the seventh was home, she waited for the solitary boarder.

This morning, Brown looked very tired. He had a bandage over his right hand, rather clumsily put on, but he made no comment about it and nor did Mrs. Tennison, who had learned that he was inclined to go silent whenever she asked personal questions.

She thrust the newspaper in front of him – the *Evening Globe*, which she fetched most mornings from the corner newspaper shop so that she could look through the fields of the day's races, and plan her small bets.

Mr. Brown blinked at the paper.

"I really don't —" he began, peering short-sightedly, and she was about to draw the paper away when he caught his breath. She thought that the most natural thing in the world, for this was a shocking affair; *eight* people burned to death.

Brown was at the table, standing up, one hand on the back of his chair. She still held the newspaper in front of his eyes. He was always pale, but now all the colour seemed to have been drained from his cheeks, his lips were parted as if the horror of what he read struck savagely at him. Mrs. Tennison had never seen anyone quite so rigid looking. After what seemed a long time, he stretched out his right hand and took the paper, put his left hand to his breast pocket for his glasses. He put them on, and Mrs. Tennison was surprised to see that his hand was trembling and the newspaper was shaking; it confirmed her judgment that Mr. Brown was a very kind, good-hearted man, deeply affected by the sufferings of others. He put his glasses on, then read the headlines and began to read the story. Suddenly, he sat down, and dropped the newspaper so that it covered the knives and forks, the plates and dishes all laid for his lunch.

"I was saying to Mr. Hulbert at the shop, it's the most terrible case I've ever heard about. *Eight* of the poor souls, and they say that some of them were actually screaming. They —"

"Don't!" cried Mr. Brown.

"I – I'm sorry if I've upset you," Mrs. Tennison said. "I can easily understand it, Mr. Brown, I'm very sorry. Why don't you try to forget about it? I've a nice little fillet of sole and a lovely pork chop —"

"I – I'm sorry," Brown said, in a choky voice. "I don't feel at all well, Mrs. Tennison. That – that story has upset me." He stood up unsteadily and pushed past her. She heard him going up to his room and by the time he was half-way up the stairs, he was almost running. His door slammed.

Mrs. Tennison stared at the newspaper, and said in a low-pitched, wondering voice:

"I wouldn't have expected it to upset him like that. If I'd known it would put him off his food, I wouldn't have brought the paper in." She stared more intently, and there was a very thoughtful look in her eyes as she went on: "I can't save the sole, I'll have to eat that myself, but the chop'll be all right, he can have that for his dinner this evening. He'll be famished by then." She picked up the newspaper and hurried out to her salvage work in the kitchen.

Upstairs in his front room overlooking Battersea Park and, in the distance, the pile of the Battersea Power Station, 'Mr. Brown' was standing by the window, staring without seeing, his eyes screwed up, his face screwed up, his hands clenched; and he kept muttering to himself.

"I thought it was an empty flat. I thought it was an empty flat. I thought it was an empty flat. I thought the people in the other flats would have plenty of time to get away. I thought . . ."

He knew, deep in his heart, that he had gone to the wrong floor – the flat immediately above had been empty. But he did not admit his error, even to himself, did not admit that he had been unable to think clearly since his wife and daughter had perished. Soon, he made a strange discovery; the agony was not so great. It was as if the death of the Millers had eased it.

Across the river, in a small house in North Islington where he lived with his elderly mother and father and his only sister, an ugly, very fat woman of thirty, a man named John Stewart Briggs was reading the *Evening Globe*. He was sitting at the kitchen table, elbows on the soiled white tablecloth, coat off, sleeves of his blue shirt rolled up over strong, brawny-looking arms which were thick with black hairs. There was something almost repulsive about the hairs on those arms because they were so coarse and matted. He was a plain man to look at, with a blunted nose and a blunted chin – a surprisingly weak-looking chin in a person of such physical strength. His eyes were small and very bright blue, deepset and buried-looking because of his shaggy black eyebrows, rather like the hairs on his arms. The hair grew low on his forehead, and was thick and shiny with grease. He badly needed a shave.

His sister was dishing up in the kitchen; his mother and father were away, visiting relations. He could hear the clatter of the dishes, and if he had cared to glance towards the scullery, would have seen the steam rising from a saucepan of cabbage.

He was oblivious of all this.

He was reading the inside page, and the account of the murder of Ivy Manson. Her picture was there, the picture of a gay and smiling child. He knew her well. She had passed this house every day for years. In fact her parents had pushed her past the house in a pram. He was a delivery van driver for a small firm of wholesalers with warehouses round the corner from here, and Ivy had often passed the van when he had been loading and delivering. Once or twice, he had given her a ride in the cabin – and that was the fact which most worried him now.

Did anyone know about those rides?

Nothing in the story suggested that the police had the slightest clue. The details were glossed over, so that people shouldn't be too shocked, and as he read he seemed to relive the whole thing, from the moment he had crept inside the house and up the stairs. He had put a cloth over the kid's face and mouth, and drawn it tight so that she couldn't see who it was, and couldn't cry out; then he had tied her hands. The cloth had slipped in her struggles, and the light from a street lamp had shone straight on to his face. He had actually seen the gleam of recognition in her eyes. That was the moment she had been done for.

He could almost feel her struggling, too.

He wiped the sweat off his forehead, and then his sister came plodding in, carrying a dish of stew with dumplings in one hand, and a bigger dish of cabbage in the other.

"Come on, Jack, put that newspaper away and start serving. Proper waste of time and money, that newspaper. You'll be a fool if you ever put a penny on a gee-gee again." She slapped the dishes down, and it was almost a miracle that she did not spill any of the stew.

Briggs folded the paper and put it aside. He ladled out stew until his own plate was overflowing, and then began to

eat with noisy heartiness. He did not look at the newspaper
again until he left for the afternoon round. Then he had it
folded to the racing guide, and spent ten minutes on the
telephone to a bookmaker before he started his deliveries.

Another man who read the newspapers with great care
that lunch time was Charles Ericson, of the firm of Ericson,
Roscoe and Banning. He did not spend much time over the
story of the fire or the murder of Ivy Manson; in fact he did
not spend much time on anything, but he studied each headline with methodical care. He was sitting alone at a small
table in the window of the dining-room of his club, a small
and exclusive dining club in the City. He was well-dressed
in the conventional black suit and striped trousers, one of
the few men who stuck to the old convention. He was in the
middle-forties, and outwardly very prosperous. He ran a
Jaguar, owned a detached house near Esher, one of the
more exclusive London dormitories, had a smart, attractive
wife·with a much keener mind than most – she had been at
Roedean and Girton – and a daughter and a son. The son
was seventeen, and beginning his last year at one of the
middle grade public schools in the west midlands; his daughter was two years older, and at a mannequin school in Paris.
Ericson earned about four thousand pounds a year, less
tax; and he spent over five thousand pounds a year.
That was why he and Roscoe had planned the share issue
so carefully, handling everything they could themselves,
arranging a cover with a firm of solicitors who were old-
fashioned enough and sufficiently impressed by the name of
Ericson and Roscoe to back the issue without taking too
much trouble to check that all was well. It was one of the
oldest tricks: Roscoe, the engineer of the partnership, had
been abroad, and had come back with some faked, or partly
faked, reports on iron ore in land owned by the company in
Central Africa. They had spent a lot of time and thought
before deciding that it should be iron. The more rewarding
and quicker yielding ores had been tempting, but had also
been more likely to be suspect. Iron had a reassuring

solidity; who would pretend that such a prosaic commodity
was there if it wasn't?

Ericson, the secretary and accountant, had had legal
training and had spent years in a broker's office some time
ago. He had worked out the details of the plot, knowing at
the time how often it had been done before. He had been
fully aware that there was a risk, but he had not expected it
to come so quickly after the issue had been floated and
heavily subscribed; investors had also been fooled by the
names of Ericson and Roscoe and the law firm acting for
them. Ericson did not yet know why the police were
suspicious, but two detectives had asked some awkward questions. The law firm had been quickly alarmed; to reassure
it, Ericson had stated flatly that so far as he knew, the whole
thing was absolutely genuine; there *was* iron ore in the range
of hills.

The police and the solicitors wanted to talk to Roscoe.
They were undoubtedly looking for him, now, but hadn't
found him yet; at least, there was no mention that they had
in the *Evening Globe*.

Ericson finished his meal with a morsel of Danish Blue, a
biscuit and some coffee, and went out into the narrow streets
of the City of London. A few acquaintances, club members
and servants nodded, smiled or bowed to him, for there was
not yet the slightest rumour in the City that anything was
wrong. If a rumour ever started, Ericson believed that he
would notice the effect at once.

It was a very pleasant, warm afternoon.

He went into his office, on the top floor of an insurance
building, where there were two ledger clerks, an assistant
surveyor, and his secretary, little Miss Goudge. No message
had come in. The police had been discreet in all their
inquiries, he knew, and were not likely to say anything to the
staff unless they felt very sure of themselves.

"I think I'll play truant for the afternoon," he said to
Miss Goudge. "If Mr. Roscoe calls from Paris, have the call
transferred to my home, will you?"

"Yes, Mr. Ericson."

"If anyone else wants me, say I'll be in tomorrow morning," added Ericson.

He went out, collected the black Jaguar from a parking lot near London Bridge, and drove home in the warmth of the afternoon. When he pulled into the private road where his house was situated, he saw his wife kneeling in front of the herbaceous border which was not yet showing much flower, although there were some clumps of polyanthus and forget-me-not, some daffodils, narcissi and grape hyacinths. Two small magnolia trees in full bloom graced the beautifully kept lawn. His wife heard the crunch of the wheels on the gravel, looked round, and immediately waved.

The only thing that Ericson had ever needed was more money. Everything else in life was exactly as he wanted it, and as he approached Joan, whose dark hair was a little rumpled, whose make-up needed repairing, but whose eyes had a glow of welcome, he felt a pang of something akin to despair.

"You're all right, darling, aren't you?" asked Joan, and he knew that she had seen the sudden change in his expression.

"Perfectly," he told her, and kissed her, and deliberately held her close to him, moving slightly to and fro so that he could feel the yielding firmness of her bosom. "It was a glorious afternoon, I thought I'd play truant and come and be spoiled. Michael *is* out, isn't he?"

Joan laughed.

"He's at the club, playing tennis, and while Joanna Sparshott is there he'll haunt the place. It won't be too long before you have a bad case of a lovesick son on your hands."

"At the moment, you have a lovesick husband," Ericson said. "How long must you spend in the garden?"

"Five minutes," Joan replied.

Then, and as he watched her, and as he lay with her, and as they sat and talked idly afterwards, the sun playing on them through the leaded panes of the bedroom window, he felt a deep need of her, and realisation that the need would become greater with the years. He was beginning to realise exactly what it would mean if the fraud became public knowledge. He found himself thinking in desperation that he must find a way of making sure that it did not. It wasn't only the thought of disgrace, there was this awful danger of being parted from Joan.

If she were surprised by his mood or by his passion, by his silences or by his trick of looking away from her, as if he could not bear to study her face more closely, she said nothing. When the telephone rang, about half past five, he started violently, and knew that she must have noticed it. He controlled himself, got up, and went to the telephone by the side of the bed.

"Charles Ericson speaking."

If this was the police —

"Hallo, Dad, you're home early!" It was Michael. "I say, four of us are making up a party for supper and a show in town tonight. I won't be home till late. Knowing how worried Mum gets if I'm late, I thought I'd better tell you."

"Fine, Michael, thanks," Ericson said.

"Everything's all right, isn't it?" asked Michael. "I mean, you don't mind. Er – it's a mixed foursome, and —"

"It includes Joanna Sparshott."

"Good lord! How did you know?"

Ericson chuckled.

"If you're going to be home much later than eleven o'clock you'd better ring again," he said. "I'll tell your mother." He put the telephone down and forced himself to smile across at Joan. He was fiercely glad that they were to be alone for the evening, for he had a presentiment that any moment some awful eruption might blast them apart.

About sixty miles away, in a small house on the outskirts of Brighton, without a view of the sea but with easy access to it, Tony Harrison breezed into the kitchen where his wife Pamela was ironing. He was always over-hearty with her; it was the only way he could keep up any pretence at being contented. Pamela remained something of an enigma to her husband; she had been for a long time. Years ago she had discovered that he could not keep his hands off other girls, and there had been a dreadful quarrel. Their first child had been on the way at the time, and he had been alarmed in case she carried out a threat to kill herself.

She had not.

But the child had seemed to reconcile her to his roaming habits, giving her an interest when he was away. Gradually they had developed a kind of double-life, Pam's with the children and the home, his partly around the cars, the dance halls and the varied amusements of the big seaside resort. With him, Pam was almost docile, submissive whenever he wished – when he made no demands she knew quite well that there was another woman – and apparently content, provided she had enough money for her own and the children's needs.

For a few years, this had satisfied Tony Harrison. In fact, during the years when their two children, a boy and a girl, were growing up, he had been contented, being genuinely fond of the children, especially Timothy. The boy was now eighteen, and had announced quite calmly, only a few months ago, that he was going to join the Army. He was already a regular soldier, stationed in the north of England, and apparently happy enough.

Then Harrison's daughter Jenny had decided to go to work in London, and came to Brighton only for an occasional week-end.

Now there was only Pamela to go home to, and Harrison not only began to hate going home to his spiritless wife and the quiet rooms, but he began to hate her. He persuaded himself that she had driven the children away from home, by making it so dull for them, the bitch, just as she had made it too dull for him. He felt bitter and vengeful, and there were times when he could have screamed at Pam, could have shouted out the hideous truth of his hate for her.

There was a dreadful irony in the situation which Harrison did not fully comprehend. To keep his home and his children, he had first committed murder.

It seemed so long ago, that he had almost forgotten what had screwed him up to the pitch of the crime, but twice since he had killed for much the same reason: a girl he had put in the family way had threatened to break up his home. He could remember one thing clearly: how cool and clear-headed he had been at the times when he had decided that this must not be allowed – for the children's sake partly, but for his own, too. Pam would get the children if she divorced him, and he would have a crippling burden of maintenance to pay.

He had killed quickly and mercifully, first kissing his unsuspecting mistress, holding the kiss, and bringing up his hands, and pressing against the windpipe. It was surprisingly quick, unconsciousness seemed to come within sixty seconds. There had been the problem of disposing of the body, but Harrison had overcome it easily enough. Not far away from the spot where he usually met his loves was a disused sand and gravel quarry, and the sides of the quarry had been filled with big holes. Some old tools had been left there, too, and he had dug a deep grave within half an hour, and buried the girl. Two years later, when it had been necessary to kill again for the same reason, the obvious place for the body had been in the old grave which had been undiscovered for two years.

It had been after this that Harrison had begun to hate Pamela, partly because she was so quiet and submissive, without any spirit, partly because it was becoming obvious by then that the children weren't likely to settle at home. It did not once occur to Harrison to blame himself; keeping the home going was Pam's job.

His third killing, of Florence Denny, had been for different reasons. She had started to blackmail him, and he had just let her have it. He could remember to this day how startled she had looked – and how he had wished that he had been squeezing Pamela's neck.

Harrison had stayed home in the evenings for a few weeks after that and Pam had been unbearable. He came to hate the sight and sound of her.

Then he had met Chloe Duval at a dance at the Gala Ballroom. At first he had seen her only as a little bit of stuff shaped rather like an egg timer, and possessed of a wiggle which suggested that she would be pretty good on the dance floor and in other places he could think of. She was exactly what he needed to relieve the monotony. Chloe had come to live in Brighton recently, all her relatives were in London, and she was running her own little flat. Everything was just as he liked, especially as she seemed to have a bit of money of her own, and did only occasional modelling. She had never said so, but he believed that she was an artist's model used to posing in the altogether, but the important point was that she had taken his mind off his problems.

He had never known anything like her, in or out of bed. Before he knew what was happening, he was desperately in love with her.

He wanted to marry her...

So he wanted Pam dead.

He had not yet made up his mind when or how to kill her, but he kept up the breezy act, to make sure she suspected nothing. Pam looked up from the ironing, and gave her patient smile.

"Hallo, dear," she said. "I didn't expect you home for lunch, but I can soon get you something."

"Sandwich and a cuppa, that's all I need," said Harrison, and he went to the ironing board, gave Pamela a perfunctory squeeze, and went on heartily: "I've got a special job on tonight, Pam. Got to take a bomb up to London for an old geezer with more dough than sense. So I'll be home late. That okay with you?"

"Yes, of course," Pamela said. "Whatever you say, dear."

He watched her go into the kitchen, and his fingers itched for her throat.

Pamela Harrison stood by the kitchen table, beating an omelette, and trying not to break down. The loneliness without the children was almost unbearable, and now Tony had started an affair with yet another woman. For years Pamela had steeled herself to put up with this kind of situation, because she loved him as much now as she always had.

She would still have to keep her self-control, she knew, would have to wait until the affair was over, but — why wasn't he satisfied with her? What did he find in these other women? Would the time never come when he would realise how much she wanted him, loved him, felt lost without him?

She was smiling demurely when she took him in a ham omelette and some fried bread. When Harrison left, just after two o'clock, he was whistling gaily at the wheel of a Riley with trade number plates on. That was the car he would collect Chloe in, later.

He had not the slightest idea that the radio service van which followed him out of the street was being driven by a policeman, but he noticed the van. He was a bright, alert man, and no fool; and the radio van puzzled him. He forgot it when he reached the showrooms, because it drove past. When he went to pick Chloe up from her flat in Hove, a post office van kept on his tail, and he noticed that without thinking very deeply about it.

Chloe opened the door, hugging a dressing-gown across her chest, and when he was inside and the door closed, she let the front of the gown fall open. That was all she was wearing.

CHAPTER V

FIRE CHIEF

CARMICHAEL'S CLUB, Gideon had soon found, was one of the older ones in a big building near the Embankment, with great high ceilings and huge marble and tiled pillars, the statues of famous men in their party, portraits of the famous, an air of quietness and almost serenity. Voices were not exactly hushed but none was raised. The service was quick and efficient without being slick and without the middle-aged waitresses being pert. The dining-room overlooked a terrace which in turn overlooked the Embankment and the Thames, about half a mile from Gideon's own office, but here the stark modern outline of the Festival Hall, and the big clock above the main building of Waterloo Station, took the place of the London County Hall.

Carmichael was a fastidious eater; Gideon a trencherman. Here the steak pudding had an appetising richness almost forgotten in the average restaurant. Carmichael picked at a grilled trout, and was rather finicky as he took the skin off. They had walked here, talking a little about the Lambeth fire, but it was not until Gideon was nearly through, all but satiated by the steak pudding, that Carmichael said :

"I wanted to see you, Gideon, because several features of the Lambeth fire seem to me – and some of my senior officers – peculiar, to say the least. Has anything in the case so far known suggested that to you?"

"The first obvious thing is that there couldn't be any insurance motive, so the probable motive was murder," Gideon said, and Carmichael nodded. There was a gleam in his pale eyes which suggested that he had something up his sleeve, and Gideon was trying to decide whether to allow him to score a little triumph, or whether to come out with the notion which had entered his own mind. He decided to let Carmichael have his moment.

"Yes," Carmichael encouraged.

"The second thing is that the firebug wasn't anyone who lived in the tenement – everyone's been accounted for, according to the report from Division."

"I didn't know that," said Carmichael. The gleam became brighter. "You may think that I am making a mountain out of a molehill, Gideon, but some of my senior officers and I have been rather puzzled by three and possibly four similar fires in the past five months."

Ah, thought Gideon. "*Other fires?*" he exclaimed.

"Yes. And arson was only seriously suspected in one of them," said Carmichael. "There was the outbreak in Bethnal Green, in November, when seven houses scheduled for demolition but still occupied were burnt down with the loss of two lives – a woman and her daughter."

"I remember that one" Gideon said. "Put it down to kids trying to make fireworks in one of the back rooms. Some sticks of dynamite they'd stolen from a dump blew up in the room, after everyone had gone to bed. Sparks from a fire according to you chaps."

"That's right," Carmichael agreed. "The next one was in Whitechapel. No person was seriously injured, but two tenement buildings, rather like those that were destroyed last night, were gutted."

"I remember," agreed Gideon. "A kitchen boiler burst, didn't it?"

"That was the theory," Carmichael answered. "The third fire was in Canning Town, and on this occasion more slum houses were destroyed. Most of the houses were already empty and scheduled for demolition, but a dozen were occupied, and the occupants all escaped in reasonable time."

Gideon said: "I think I'm beginning to see what you're driving at."

"I didn't think it would take you long," the Fire Chief said dryly. He glanced round, beckoned a waiter, and went on: "What will you have to follow? A sweet, or some cheese – or both if you feel inclined."

"That golden pudding with syrup I saw you with just now looks good," Gideon said to the waiter.

"It's always very good sir."

"I wish I had half your appetite," Carmichael complained. "Bring me a small caramel pudding, and then we'll both see the cheese board." The waiter went off, and Carmichael continued with the subject of fires as if there had been no interruption. "The fourth fire was in a similar area near Bethnal Green. All of them have been in slum areas, you will realise, and in buildings which were scheduled for or should have been scheduled for demolition. There is one other factor which you may not have any reason to be cognisant of."

"Go on," said Gideon.

"After each of these fires, and as far as I have been able to judge, only after these, a call has been made to the nearest fire station by someone who has dialled 999 and asked for the Fire Service without giving a name. The caller has spoken to the operator in charge, given the exact seat of the fire, and rung off without further explanation. In each case there was a comment by the operator: *'Suspected hoax,'* because of the calmness of the caller – most genuine reports are hurried and excited. You know that we have more false alarms than genuine calls, don't you?"

Gideon nodded.

"My attention was first drawn to the fact that these were all slum fires, and that no motive could readily be seen," Carmichael said. "Moreover, there was a rational explanation of how they started except in the one in Canning Town, where petrol was known to have been taken to the scene of the outbreak. Even then there was a suggestion that someone was using the empty houses as an unofficial warehouse, and kept petrol on the premises. We can now prove that last night's fire was due to arson, and each of the other cases could have been. Last night, also, there was a telephone call from a call-box some ten minutes walk away from the seat of the fire. The caller explained exactly where the fire was, and rang off. Now it was quite impossible for anyone to have seen the fire from that call-box, Gideon, and there are dozens nearer the seat of the fire."

"Sure?" asked Gideon, sharply.

"I am positive."

"I'll take your word for it," Gideon said, and watched Carmichael instead of starting on the golden pudding, oozing with syrup, which was placed in front of him. "I'll take your word for it that these jobs could be by the same firebug, too. Can you let me have all the reports you've got, down to the smallest detail, and arrange for one of your chaps to contact us at the Yard? I'll put Margetson on the job, he's our best man on arson."

"I'll do everything I can to assist you," Carmichael promised, and smiled quite broadly. "In my brief-case I have copies of all the files, I felt sure that you would not want a great deal of persuading."

"Any more theories?" asked Gideon.

"I think it's a little early for that," Carmichael demurred, "but if there is any connection between the series of fires in slum areas, well – it *could* be that you are faced with a fanatic who sees it as a kind of duty to take action more

quickly than the authorities. We have had several such
people to deal with, and usually they are soon caught. I
have often wondered what a really clever man could achieve
if he were driven by that compulsion. That is why I felt I
should discuss the situation with you. We are very proud of
our welfare state and our slum clearance programmes,"
went on the Fire Chief, "but you probably know as well as
I do how shocking the conditions are in a great number of
districts. I was studying the statistics the other day. My
Department regards the fire risk in central and east and
south-east London as twice as great as that in any other
residential district, due entirely to old buildings and old
properties where there are no satisfactory precautions against
fire, where there is grave overcrowding, where in some cases
water is only laid on to one floor of a house. We are nothing
like as civilised and advanced as we like to think. But don't
let that concoction on your plate get cold."

"No, I won't," said Gideon. He picked up his spoon and
plunged it into the gooey mess, which was exactly what he
liked, while he concentrated on Carmichael's theory. He
could recall several cases of fire-raising by men with twisted
minds, not always with a material motive – sometimes
simply because the perpetrator liked to see things burn.

When he finished eating, his mouth was tacky, but
there was some pale ale left in the glass. He drank it.
"I've been wondering," he went on musingly, "whether the
places which have been burned are owned by the same
people."

"I can't really say," said Carmichael, and his eyes showed
his interest. "You think that it could be an attack on an
owner who is making money out of these appalling conditions?"

"Don't know what I think yet," replied Gideon. "You
put the idea into my head."

He was still pondering at three o'clock that afternoon,
when he sent for Chief Inspector Margetson. Margetson
was a middle-aged man who might reasonably have had a
grievance against the Yard's promotion system; he had little
or no book-learning, so there was no examination that he

could pass. His spelling was atrocious, and anyone looking at his hand-written reports must have believed that they were written by a schoolboy. Reading them gave a different impression; they were models of conciseness, and the difficult and technical words were always accurately spelt. "Even I can use a dictionary sometimes," Margetson would say. His spelling and his lack of academic knowledge would stop him from further promotion; only stringent efforts by Gideon and others who knew his quality had pushed him into the inspectors' ranks. He was a chunky man of medium height, his face had deep lines and some of the chasms in it defied the electric razor which he always used a few hours later than he should. His straw-coloured hair was badly cut, partly because it seemed to grow in several directions; he boasted cheerfully of having three crowns.

"No wonder I'm lucky," he would say; so he became 'Lucky' Margetson.

He tapped on the door of Gideon's office, and when Gideon called 'come in', entered with caution, closed the door with care, and gave the impression that he wondered what he was on the carpet for.

"Hallo, Lucky, take a pew," Gideon invited, and a face which until then had been set in lines of uncertainty changed to one like a beaming schoolboy's. Nothing about Margetson's face was quite even; one side of his mouth was higher than the other, one nostril was more pinched than the other, his eyes were slightly different shades of greeny-brown.

"That's a relief," he said, and pulled up a chair. "I thought you had eyes at the back of your head, Mr. Gideon."

"What have you done wrong now?"

"Went over and had a look at the Lambeth job this morning when I was out on that warehouse arson fix. You can tie that one up and put it in your pocket." Margetson's voice was a much more pronounced Cockney even than Lemaitre's, yet he chose his words with care. "Insurance job, the storage firm is right in the red. I've put in my report."

"Good. What took you over to Lambeth?"

"Bloody funny thing," said Margetson. "I was going to

have a word with Joe Bell about it. Bell was out of the
office for once. Fifth slum fire in five months."

"If you'd told me about it this morning, I could have
passed it on to Carmichael of the Fire Service, instead of
having him tell me," said Gideon, dryly.

"He on to it? No flies on Carmichael, I must say. Well,
send me for a brown ale," exclaimed Margetson. "How
much did he know? About the warning telephone calls?"

"Yes."

"That's what puzzled me first. Went over to have a look
at the call-box used last night – that's one good thing, when
they use a kiosk you can check back," Margetson said. "The
operators know all the call-box numbers. This one's at the
corner of Sussex Street and Hemp Road, mile and a half
from Hilton Terrace. Seventeen public call-boxes are
within a mile radius, so it wasn't used because it was the
nearest. I borrowed a bike from the Divisional chaps and
cycled round to Hilton Terrace four different ways, the only
ways you can go," the chunky man went on. "Unless there
was a blaze showing against the sky you couldn't have seen
that fire until you were practically on the spot. My guess is
that the chap who startled it cycled off and phoned a warning when he felt sure he couldn't be copped. So he wasn't
simply a man who enjoyed watching a fire."

"Any ideas about why he should give a warning!" Gideon
asked.

"No, sir," answered Margetson. "I'm not sticking my
neck out that far. Could be he just likes lighting fires. When
you get down to it, that's usually the answer. Funny thing,
one of my own kids is a little terror. Put him anywhere near
a match-box and he has to strike a match and start a blaze.
Tanned his hide only last week, I did, but when you come to
think of it, most kids are the same – if they're not scared stiff
of fire they love playing with it. And not everybody grows
up, do they, Commander?"

"I see what you mean. Have you checked the ownership
of the different places that were burnt down?"

"No," answered Margetson, and his eyes rounded, his lips
formed an 'O'. "Strewth, what made me miss that one? As

a matter of fact, I haven't really given it much thought, just kind of wondered. The Lambeth do gave me a jolt."

"All right, Lucky," Gideon said, and handed over the duplicate files Carmichael had given him. "Call your contact man at the Fire Service H.Q., Carmichael's already briefed him. Dig as deep as you can. You're looking for evidence of arson, motive, ownership of the property concerned, any other common factors – such as, are there relations living in these different places? Check all the possibilities, and don't go to sleep on it."

"I won't go to sleep," Margetson promised earnestly. "How about the Lambeth job?"

"It's yours, with the Division."

"Ta," said Margetson, and put such feeling into the simple word that it told Gideon how much he had been hoping to be put in charge.

"Tell Joe Bell if you want to see me at any time," Gideon added. "Give this one priority."

"After eight deaths it'll get all I've got, day and night," Margetson promised. "Funny how it gets you when kids are involved, isn't it? Had any luck with that swine out at Islington?"

"No."

"Don't talk to me about abandoning capital punishment," said Margetson. "Thanks again, Mr. Gideon." He got up, nearly kicked his chair over, and blundered out. Gideon was smiling faintly when he turned back to his desk and the mass of reports which had come in since half past twelve, and he began to read each one, quickly but thoroughly. He heard a footstep outside, the door opened and Bell came in – and Gideon's telephone rang. He lifted it while staring at reports on the watch smuggling investigation.

"Gideon."

"Yes, put him through. It's Cornish," he said in an aside to Bell. "Hallo, Cornish . . . Eh?"

Cornish had a note of resignation in his deep voice.

"It was the same patched hole in the same glove – the one in the bank tunnel last week and the one at Bournemouth way back. Just thought you'd like to know you were right."

"Going to get you anywhere?" asked Gideon.

"Wouldn't be surprised," said Cornish. "I'm going to have another go at the chap we have caught, named Lenny Clapper. When he knows we've tied it up with the Bournemouth job he might think we know more than we do, and there's one other thing." Gideon had been sure that there would be, because nothing Cornish had yet said would justify this call. "Wouldn't like to put any money on this, George, but that hole in the glove set me wondering. Remember we picked up the gun used on the night watchman out at Brentford, six months ago?"

Gideon said heavily: "Yes, I do."

"Same kind of mark on the gun as there is here and there was at Bournemouth," Cornish told him. "I didn't handle the Brentford job, but I remembered talking about the impression to Lemaitre, who did. I dug out the photographs of the print taken off the gun. Same one all right. So that means we're up against a hardened killer."

"You be careful, then," Gideon ordered.

"I'll be careful all right. See what it means, don't you?"

"Tell me."

"It explains why Lenny Clapper hasn't talked. He'd rather take what's coming to him for this job, say seven years in chokey, rather than talk and get himself life – or put himself in bad with the man who killed that night watchman. This could be a very nasty job."

"Very," Gideon agreed grimly. "What you want now is the name of anyone known to use violence and also on Clapper's list of acquaintances. Talked to Mrs. Clapper?"

"All she says is that she doesn't know a thing and doesn't believe her husband would do such a thing," Cornish answered.

"Why don't you try to scare her?" asked Gideon. "Bring her along here for questioning, say. If I go and bellow, it might frighten the wits out of her. How long will it take you to get her here?"

"Ought to be able to fix it by half past five," answered Cornish. "Might be a good idea. Thanks, George."

"I'll be here," Gideon said. "Before you go, though – if the same glove was used two years ago, it'd be threadbare by now, wouldn't it?"

"Don't give me that," protested Cornish. "If these boys get a good pair of flexible gloves they can work in, they look after them like pearls. Old Tommy Ledbetter used the same pair for nine years, and he —"

"All right, have it your own way," Gideon conceded, and Cornish hung up.

Bell was putting the finishing touches to a report. Gideon sat back in his swivel chair, leaning backwards so that his head touched the wall, and for the first time that day he put his hand into his pocket and began to smooth the rounded bowl of his large pipe, one he seldom smoked but which was nearly always in that pocket. He did not think of the fact that the sky had started to cloud over, and it was colder in the office than it had been. He wasn't thinking of Bell, nor was he really concentrating on any one of the investigations in hand. He was uneasy, and knew exactly why.

It was one thing to investigate a clear-cut job, in which the crime had already been committed. It was another to be working against people who might commit crime after crime until they were caught. If there was a connecting thread among these fires, for instance, if the same man had started them, where would he strike next? Every fireraiser had a touch of insanity, unless he was working for an insurance pay-off. Lucky Margetson had put a finger on the spot: firebugs hadn't developed in that part of their mind which was fascinated by fire. Whatever the motive, any man who could start five such conflagrations was mentally unstable – and so there was no telling what he might do next. Moreover, looking for a madman was ten times more difficult than looking for a criminal working for gain. This firebug – still assuming that it was all the work of one person – might be living a normal family life in some respectable home, might appear quite sane to those who lived and worked with him.

How could one seek a madman who crept about at night

with fire in his hands, and was simply one of London's eight millions?

How could anyone make sure that he would not start another fire with even more dreadful consequences?

And how was it possible to make sure that there wouldn't be another Ivy Manson case tonight – a child sleeping peacefully, and being bestially attacked?

How did one make sure that another night watchman wasn't shot and killed by the man who wore a cotton glove with a small darn in it?

There was only the one way to make sure of all these things: finding the criminals. In each case, the burden of responsibility upon the Yard was very great. One more attack on a child; one more fire; one more murder by a gunman; and by the very nature of its position the Force would have to carry the stigma and the guilt of failure. Because he was the Executive Chief of the Department mainly concerned, that responsibility would devolve upon him. There were plenty of officers at the Yard who would refuse to admit this, who would say that their responsibility and his stopped at putting the best they could into their job, but the truth went much further than these men realised. Supposing one of them made a mistake? Supposing Lucky Margetson had delayed making a report to him – as he almost certainly would have done – and there had been another fire tonight? Whose 'fault' would that have been? Lucky's, because he had not wanted to make a fool of himself by submitting speculation for consideration? Or his, Gideon's, for not making sure that every man who had Lucky's kind of mind came to see him, or at least sent a written report, on all such conjectures?

Rogerson, the Assistant Commissioner for Crime, would call all of this a policy of perfection. Well, why not aim for it?

One thing Gideon could not escape, and that was the feeling of uncertainty and anxiety which would grow in him like a canker until all three problems were solved and all three criminals under arrest. There were other matters, too, the countless crimes that were taking place and being planned within the area of the Metropolitan Police and of which he knew nothing. At least he need not blame himself for any of them, but tomorrow might bring as much as today in the way of horror and anxiety.

He didn't like today at all.

He liked it no better after seeing Clapper's wife, a young, well-dressed, nice-made-up woman with a flouncing walk and a brassy manner. Her Lenny wouldn't commit any crime, she declared, she didn't believe he would for a single moment.

Gideon did not need to tell Cornish to have the woman followed.

Kate was out when he arrived home and only Malcolm, the youngest of their six children was home, struggling with homework and conscience, for there was a sporting pro-gramme on television. Gideon was satisfied to sit, watch, think, and make mental notes of all that he wanted to do next day. When Kate came in, just before eleven o'clock, bright-eyed after a quick walk from the bus stop, Gideon felt the satisfaction and the glow of well-being she always contrived to give. But when they were upstairs, undressing, he heard the warning bell of a fire-engine in a nearby street, and his thoughts flew to the tenement fire and to all that this alarm might mean.

CHAPTER VI

WIFE AND UNDERSTANDING

ABOUT half past eleven that night, when the Gideons were getting into bed and while Michael Ericson was up in his room, whistling a song which his father and mother had never heard, Ericson knew that there would be no sleep for him or Joan until he had talked to her about Roscoe and the fraudulent shares. The evening had been bitter-sweet. Joan had realised a long time ago that he was worried but hadn't questioned him, it would not be fair to wait any longer before telling her what might happen. The vivid comprehension of the fact that imprisonment would mean separation from her, and the barrenness of despair which followed, had done more to depress and to worry him than anything else. She was out in the kitchen, cutting up some pieces of fish for the cat, for in spite of the five thousand a year it cost them to live, they had no living-in maid.

He heard her call: "Tibby, come along, Tibby." A draught cut in as she opened the kitchen door. "Tibby-Tibby-Tibby!" There was a pause, before she talked to the cat in the half endearing, half amused way which she had with it. The doors closed, and she came briskly from the kitchen into the living-room, with its beautifully brocaded curtains, its luxury furniture, the décor which she had carried out herself only last year, but which had cost a small fortune. In fact that had been the period of final over-spending, and the time the plot had been hatched with Roscoe.

Joan looked bright-eyed but not tired, and Ericson had not seen her so lovely for a long time, although that might be because of the way he was seeing her. It wasn't altogether, of course; the middle-forties suited her. She was justly proud of the fact that she was still slim and shapely at the waist and slender at the hips, and she had quite beautiful legs. She came across and sat on a pouffe in front of him, hugging her knees.

"Coming up, darling?"

"Yes, I think I will," said Ericson.

"Going to have a night cap?"

"Like one?"

"A teeny-weeny," she said. "I'll get it." She jumped up, and her own daughter could not move with greater suppleness or freedom. Ericson watched her as she picked up the whisky decanter, and poured out, splashed soda into both glasses, and turned round.

'Joan," he said, "I've got to talk to you."

She brought him the drink. "Yes, I know, darling." She stood over him, and as he took the drink, her hand touched his. They were not a demonstrative couple when passion was spent, and they would not be demonstrative now. "I hoped you wouldn't make me ask you what was worrying you."

"How long have you guessed?"

"I suppose for the past five or six weeks," Joan replied and sat on the pouffe again, tucking her legs under. "Don't hate me, but at first I thought it was The Other Woman."

"Good God!"

"Shocked, darling?"

"Shocked?" Ericson echoed, and laughed, actually feeling lighter-hearted than he had for a long time. "Not exactly, but it hadn't occurred to me that you might even suspect —" He broke off, tossed half the drink down, put the glass on a table by his side, and leaned forward. "God knows how you'll hate me when you know what I've done, but at least you can be sure that there hasn't been another woman, even for five minutes, since we met."

"I think I knew that, too, once I was over the first base suspicions," said Joan. "Is it business?"

"In a way."

"Are we broke?"

That question made him think that whatever she suspected, she did not dream of the truth. 'Are we broke?' A year ago, that was exactly what it had amounted to; they had been broke, he had owed ten thousand pounds but they were civil debts, the worst that could have happened had been bankruptcy. He had shied away from it with horror, like a bloody fool.

"Are we, Charles?" Her voice was gently insistent.

He could not bring himself to answer immediately, it was as if the words stuck in his throat, choking him. He saw the beginning of a frown at Joan's forehead, and the first shadows in her eyes, as if at last she began to suspect that it might not be as simple as she had made it sound. She didn't speak again, and he brushed his hand over his wet, warm forehead, moistened his lips, and made himself say:

"I wish that were all."

"I think I can take it," Joan said. "How bad is it, darling?"

"Very bad."

"Have you —" She broke off, looked up at him for a long time, and said: "Is this anything to do with Jimmy going away?"

"Yes."

"Was that issue of shares fraudulent?" Joan asked.

Ericson was so astounded that he darted back in his chair, hands raised, lips parted. Joan sipped her whisky and put the glass down, but didn't get up.

"So it was," she said, slowly, painfully.

"How – how on earth —" Ericson gave up.

"I suppose I've always been worried about that issue of shares," Joan said. "It came at such a convenient time, didn't it? I knew that we weren't doing too well. Twice last year you checked the home accounts very closely, and you've never done that before. I just had an uneasy kind of feeling." She fell silent, but still looked at him. "Whose idea was it?" When he didn't answer, she went on heavily: "I suppose it doesn't really matter, all that matters is trying to put things right. How – how much is involved?"

"About fifty thousand pounds," Ericson told her.

He saw the colour receding from her cheeks, and the shadows go dark in her eyes. She actually closed her eyes for a moment, and he realised what an awful shock this must be, in spite of the fact that she had been half-prepared. Fifty thousand pounds stated baldly like that, was a shock in itself. Oh, God, what had got into him?

She opened her eyes wide, and her voice was quite free from emotion.

"How much could we raise if we – if we sold everything, Charles? I mean *everything*. My coat and stoles, for instance, and my jewellery."

"Possibly, ten thousand," Ericson answered. He had reckoned it up time and time again.

"Would that help to – to stave things off?"

"No," said Ericson. "No, I don't really think so. It – it's a question of an investigation, if the police go any further."

"Further?"

"They've questioned me several times, and old Hailey-bury of the law firm is terrified. It's really only a question of – of the police proving that Jimmy's surveyor's reports were falsified. I've a nasty feeling that they are already having another survey made. For the time being, Jimmy's gone to earth, so that they can't question him."

"Is it *ab*solutely hopeless?" asked Joan, and at last she stood up; but she did not start pacing the room, simply went to the sideboard and poured herself another drink, then turned round to face him. "Surely —" she broke off.

"I think it's hopeless," Ericson said firmly. "I've kept fooling myself that it wasn't, that we could get away with it by claiming that the issue was made in the honest belief that the iron was in the hills, but when I think dispassionately, I have to admit that the story won't fool the police. If we had fifty thousand to pay back, withdrawing the issue because we've discovered an error in the report, it might conceivably save the day. But even if we had to do that, the firm would be finished."

"I'm not very worried about the firm." Joan surprised him now by being so brisk and matter-of-fact. "It's been a real anxiety ever since your father died, he was the only business man among the board, darling." She said that as if she had always known it. "The firm can go to pot so far as I'm concerned, but – what's the worst that would happen if the worst *did* happen?"

After a tense pause, Ericson said: "I should think seven years' imprisonment."

She drew in her breath very sharply.

"I know how it must hurt," Ericson said, trying desperately to keep his voice steady and his hands from trembling, for now the awfulness was sinking in. "I wish that were all, too, but imagine how they'll dress this up in court. Fraudulent issue on a fraudulent claim, fifty thousand one-pound shares from small investors." He stopped, clenched his hands, and felt his voice breaking. "The worst part about it is that it's true. There *were* a lot of small investors. There always are. And the newspaper reports would start immediately. Then there'd be the trial and everything it means for you, and for Michael and Joanna. I've spent night after night trying to think of a way out, but I don't think there is one." His lips puckered. "And I don't think I can face —"

"Charles!" Joan exclaimed, and moved sharply towards him. He had never seen her looking quite like this. There was anger in her eyes, and colour burning in her cheeks. Her voice was very sharp, angry. "Don't talk like that. Don't ever say it or think it. You're just forty-five. If the worst came to the worst and you had to go to prison for seven years, you would only be fifty-two when you came out. Don't talk a lot of emotional nonsense about not being able to stand it. You'll have to stand it. We all will. You may think that the disgrace will hurt the children, but how much worse would they feel if they had to live with the fact that their father had committed suicide?"

She was standing over him, commandingly. He put his hands out, blindly. She took them but stood very still and erect.

"You see that, Charles, don't you?"

"Yes," he mumbled, and hated the fact that his eyes were wet with tears and his voice was hoarse. "Yes, you're quite right, Joan. I – I've been beside myself for too long."

"I don't mind what you do, I don't mind what happens, I don't mind what we have to give up, but don't let me live in fear that you might kill yourself," Joan said.

"No," he managed to assure her, and after a pause he added bitterly: "I doubt if I would have had the guts, any-how. I haven't had many, have I? If I'd faced —"

"Listen, darling," Joan said, and a note of desperation sharpened her voice. "Supposing we don't talk about what might have been, but just face up to the situation. Are you expecting the police to – to charge you soon?"

"They might."

"Isn't there any way you can start paying back and —" She broke off, released his hands, and went back to the pouffe. When she sat down, he saw how bright her eyes were and realised that she too had been very close to tears;

and for the first time, he understood the great strength in her. "There must be some way that we can persuade Hailey-bury and the police that it wasn't fraud. You haven't admitted anything, have you?"

"No, of course not. But —"

"Couldn't Jimmy have made a genuine mistake?"

"I wish we could pretend that was a way out, but it isn't. He faked surveyor's reports. He stated that he had checked the reports in person, and that the vein of ore showed a one in ten iron content."

"Who has those reports now?"

"The police."

"Oh," said Joan, as if that made her realise how desperate the situation was. But she didn't look away, and after a while she went on stubbornly: "You've got to *try*, Charles, somehow. I think it's a mistake for Jimmy to run away and hide. If the police realise that he's hiding from them, they'll only make it worse for you. Surely the house, my furs, the jewels, everything we have is worth more than ten thousand pounds."

"To buy, they're worth twenty. To sell it's a different matter."

"Darling, I think we'll have to sleep on it, but I believe that we should bring Jimmy back, tell the police that it was a genuine mistake, and promise that the firm will pay back every penny," Joan declared. "After all, the important thing is to pay the money back and make sure that no one loses." When he didn't reply, she went on flatly: "I can't believe that the police or anyone else would want to be vindictive. Why should they? If we sell everything, and offer that as part repayment – if we make an official statement that our surveys were based on erroneous reports and that all the money will be repaid within a certain period —"

"Joan, even if the authorities could let us get away with it, we haven't got the money. Don't you understand that? I've spent every penny. The firm was in debt, I was in debt – why I couldn't raise a thousand pounds except on your things. Listen, Joan. This is my fault, and I've asked for it.

There's no reason why you should have to lose everything. You've had the furs and the jewels for years, and —"

"Don't be silly," Joan said, impatiently. "I couldn't go around in mink and diamonds if you were in prison – I would have to sell most of them to live, anyhow, I can't imagine any job I could do that would earn much money. We've got to value everything we possess, to find ways and means of borrowing or raising the money, so that the people who bought the shares can sell them back to us at par. One obvious possibility is Uncle Reggie, he *might* have a few thousand to spare, and if he has he'll lend it to us." There was a brighter light in her eyes. "Then there's Maude. She and Arthur are stinking rich, there are no two ways about it. Can we tell them? Can we say that you were misled by the reports, and that your whole reputation is at stake? I know it would mean that we'd be in debt for life to them, but they've so much money that it wouldn't really matter. I think I can help to handle Maude."

She broke off.

Ericson's eyes were shimmering with tears.

She got up and went to him, sat on the arm of his chair and slid her arm round his shoulders.

"Don't let it get you down, darling."

"Get me *down*," exclaimed Ericson in a choky voice.

In Islington, about the same time, a husband and wife were sitting together, in the small front room of their small front flat in a narrow street. There were two bedrooms, this room, the kitchen and scullery; they shared a landing bathroom with a neighbour. Here the wallpaper was of a garish red and yellow, a zig-zag pattern which their elder daughter – who had married and gone to live in Australia – had liked. On the table in the middle of the room was a green chenille tablecloth, and on this a tray with a milk drink, and some tea and milk. In the corner was a twelve-inch television set, silent and blank. The two shabby but comfortable arm-chairs were facing each other across the fireplace, with its bright green tiles and its black hearth. The only light came from a hanging lamp with a tasselled shade. Behind the chairs was the kitchen door, beyond the kitchen their dead child's bedroom. Thanks to the kindliness of neighbours and the wisdom of the authorities, the child's body had quickly been taken away from the flat.

The woman, Doris Manson, was sitting in one chair. Her husband, Mortimer, was sitting on the arm, a work-calloused hand resting on his wife's shoulders, broad fingers looking stubby, nails broken and split. They were a middle-aged couple; Ivy had been a late child and their great joy.

"Doris, it's no use just sitting there, you've got to come to bed," urged Manson. "I know how terrible you feel, honestly I do, but it's no use sitting there. It won't – it won't bring her back, Doris. Don't you understand that? Try to, dear, try to, please."

The bereaved mother did not speak or move.

"Doris, you've got to come to bed! I'll bring you some more to drink, and you must have two of those tablets the doctor left. They will help you to sleep."

The mother did not speak or move.

"Doris!" The man's voice broke, and his arm tightened on her shoulders. "Don't you think it's bad enough for me already?" Tears began to flood into his eyes. "She was the apple of my eye, you know she was. I had wonderful hopes for our Ivy, she was such a lovely girl, there wasn't a lovelier girl living. I can't believe that she's gone for ever, any more than you can. Every time I come into a room I think I hear her voice, I think I see her smiling at me, but – but we've got to face it, Doris!" He shook his wife almost wildly. "Don't you understand, we've got to pull ourselves together, it's no use giving way."

He could not go on, and he could not shake her any more; and she neither moved nor spoke.

After a while, he got up, pressed his hand tightly against his forehead, and went into the kitchen. The door leading to the little bedroom beyond was closed and locked, as the police had left it, but it seemed to open, and his beloved child seemed to appear in the doorway, wearing a dressing-gown high at the neck, her silky yellow hair beautifully brushed, her blue eyes so bright and her lips so sweet and pink.

"Oh, God, I can't stand it, I can't stand it!" he cried.

After a few minutes, he went back. His wife was sitting in exactly the same position, staring straight in front of her. Her face was drawn and her eyes were narrowed, her hands were folded in her lap. The awful thing was that she looked like Ivy.

He was startled by a tap at the front door, and after a moment, went and opened it. It was an elderly woman, the neighbour across the landing.

"Hallo, Mr. Manson," she said, quietly. "I thought I saw a light under the door, and I couldn't rest until I'd made sure you're all right. How is Mrs. Manson?"

"She – she – she just won't say a word. She's been like it for hours, ever since they took my darling away." Manson's voice was almost at breaking point.

"Let me see if I can do anything with her," offered the neighbour. "And why don't you go across and lie down for an hour on our sofa, Mr. Manson? Bert's expecting you, I told him I thought I could guess how things were. I might be able to help your wife, and it certainly won't do any good if you knock yourself up."

Her husband appeared in the other doorway.

Manson went across, slowly, gratefully, fearfully.

Some distance from north Islington and farther from Esher, the widow of Police Constable Jarvis lay alone in the large double bed, not really finding it strange to be alone, because Tom had been on night duty so often. In a peculiar way she had to remind herself that this was different, that the night would never come when he would lie beside her again, snoring with familiar faintness much of the time. There would be no more moments when he would become the lover she had known in the early days of their marriage, and even before it. He had always seemed so quiet, pipe and slippers, television and dog, garden and the occasional pint of beer; sometimes weeks would go by when it was almost possible to forget that she had a husband, only just a snoring sleeping partner; and then for a few almost abandoned days, usually after he had come off a spell of night duty, there would be nothing she could do with him. That was why she had taken such definite precautions; if he had had his reckless way, they would have had a dozen children, not three.

She heard a sound in a bedroom across the hall, and turned her head towards the door which she had left ajar in case any of the children woke. She had not yet told them the truth, only that their father had been badly injured, and was in hospital. Now, her heart began to thump with the anticipated dread of the inevitable moment when they would have to know all the truth.

A door creaked.

"Hester! Is that you?" She stretched out a firm arm, and put on the beside lamp, which dimmed the pale light coming from the street lamp at the window. This was a small, two storied house, built between the wars in a pleasant little suburb; Eltham.

There were footsteps, the door opened, and Hester the eldest child stood framed in it. She was a big girl for ten years old, and already beginning to mature physically. She wore pyjamas of faded pink stockinette, a little too tight for her, with a T-shirt neck. Her hair was drawn straight back from her forehead, which helped to give her an older look. Her brown eyes, always large and very like her father's, seemed huge and luminous.

The clock downstairs struck twelve.

"Can't you get to sleep?" asked Mrs. Jarvis, and hitched herself up in bed. "Come in with me for a few minutes, pet, you'll soon drop off."

The girl came eagerly, scrambling on to the bed, but the moment she was lying down and looking at her mother, she was more subdued.

"Worried about Daddy?" asked Mrs. Jarvis, and somehow managed to keep her voice calm.

"Yes, I am," Hester answered. "Mummy —" She broke off, but did not look away, although there was something in her manner which told Mrs. Jarvis that she really had some trouble on her mind.

"Yes, pet?"

"You – you know I went to the corner shop to get some extra tea and sugar."

"Of course I do."

"Mummy," said Hester, in a very small voice, "as I went in the shop they stopped talking, all of a sudden. Mrs. Wagner was there, and Auntie Flo. But they hadn't seen me at first, and I heard them say that Daddy was dead." There was another long, tense pause, before she went on: "*Is* he?"

Mrs. Jarvis tried not to close her eyes, tried not to show any signs of breaking down. In the moment which elapsed between question and answer, she wondered how this disaster would affect Hester, the one child who worried her. The others, aged seven and four, would not suffer so much, but Hester – it had always been difficult to understand the child, who showed no preference between her mother and father, but was always a little remote, a little too self-sufficient.

"I'm afraid it is true, darling," Mrs. Jarvis managed to say steadily.

Hester's brown eyes seemed to grow enormous.

"I knew it," she said, softly. "I had a feeling that he was, it was the way you looked when you told us about the accident. I knew it must be serious, or Aunt Mabel wouldn't have come to look after us while you were at the hospital, and when you came home and said you weren't going to the hospital any more today, I thought: That means Daddy is dead. Why didn't you tell me right away?"

Her mother said: "It is a terribly hard thing to believe even for me, darling, and I wanted – I wanted to feel strong enough to talk to you about it."

"I see," said Hester, and after another long pause, she went on: "You and Daddy don't believe in life after death, do you?"

That almost made the mother break down, but she managed to answer:

"It isn't that we don't believe, it's rather that we're not convinced. We keep an open mind on it."

"Well, Daddy knows now," said Hester, thoughtfully. "Would you mind telling me one more thing?"

"If I can, I will."

"Did he *suffer* much?"

"For a few minutes I'm afraid he did," answered Mrs. Jarvis and she would never know how she kept herself from bursting into tears. Her nerves were almost beyond screaming point. "But there was a doctor on the scene very quickly, and modern drugs are wonderful pain-killers. It didn't last long."

"And was he a hero?"

"Yes, he was a very brave man, Hester."

"I always thought he was," declared Hester. She blinked, and her eyes misted over as if the stimulant of question and answer were beginning to lose their effect. She lay still for several minutes, breathing evenly, and her mother was glad to lie on her back, eyes closed, burning tears forcing their way through. Then sleepily, Hester asked: "Mummy, you know that there's to be the special school outing next Friday."

"Yes, pet."

"Will this make any difference. Can I still go?"

Oh, God.

"Of course you can still go."

"Thank you," said Hester; and ten minutes later she was fast asleep, so soundly that she did not hear her mother's convulsive sobbing. She would never know that she had broken her mother's tension, either, and that out of the paroxysm there was born some ease of mind.

Hester woke again a little after seven o'clock in the morning. Neil, her four-year-old brother, was running about his bedroom. Hester pushed back the bedclothes and was at the door when her mother woke.

"I'll see to him," she promised.

Mrs. Jarvis sat up slowly, looked at herself in the mirror, saw the dried traces of tears on her cheeks, remembered that last question from Hester, the one which revealed how little the child had yet been seared by the tragedy.

Then she head Neil giggling.

"The best thing to do is get them off to school," Mrs.

Jarvis said aloud, and got out of bed. Behave as if everything was normal. "Hester!" she called. "When you've
washed, start washing Neil, will you?"

"All right, Mum," Hester called back.

Pamela Harrison lay wide awake in her lonely bed at
Brighton. Tony hadn't come home, and she doubted
whether he would, tonight. He would tell her some plausible
story tomorrow, and she would have to pretend to believe it.

In Chloe's bed, lying drowsily, Harrison was going over
possible methods of murdering his wife without being
caught. One way kept recurring; she could commit suicide
because the children had left home, because he was away so
often. Suicide was the answer, but – how?

CHAPTER VII

VISITS FROM GIDEON

GIDEON woke early that morning, possibly because the
ringing of the fire alarm had been in his mind most of
the night; twice he had lain awake for several minutes,
listening to Kate's even breathing, but each time he had
dropped off quickly. Rain was scudding against the window,
and now and again a gust of wind shook a loose window on
the landing. Must put that right, Gideon thought. Never
seem to get a minute, these days. It was a little after seven.
He got up, slid his arms into a dressing-gown, and five
minutes later went to examine the landing window. None of
the children was up. Their six were down to four, now, with
Tom long since married and Prudence married to her Peter
towards the end of last year. There were no signs that
Priscilla, now nearly twenty-one, was thinking of settling
down, but Matthew, the second oldest boy, would be going
to Cambridge in a few weeks. He had worked himself to
his limit to win a scholarship. Penelope at sixteen was still

devoted to her piano, and had some promise, and young Malcolm, at thirteen, was no problem at all.

The window, of the sashcord type, rattled noisily when Gideon pushed it; a sliver of wood was needed on the sides to stop that; that meant having the window out, and might mean a sashcord renewal. "I'll do that on Saturday somehow," he said. "Must remember to get some thin slats." He went downstairs to the kitchen, and was surprised to find Matthew, tousle-haired but with his face freshly scrubbed, making the morning tea.

"Hallo, Dad."

"My, my," said Gideon. "It's not often you get up in the middle of the night. What's on your conscience?"

"Nothing, really," said Matthew. He was a smaller edition of Gideon in features, but would never have his father's breadth of shoulder or thickness of chest. He was broadening out, though, and nearly as much man as boy; as a child, he had been the family ugly duckling. "I haven't been sleeping too well, lately, that's all," he added.

Gideon looked at him thoughtfully, and saw him glance out of the kitchen window, into the small back garden with its postage-stamp lawn, the neat flower beds all round it, one a herbaceous border, another filled with wallflowers, tulips and forget-me-nots, with only the little blue flower out.

"You want to slacken off a bit," Gideon advised. "I'll take the tea up, old chap. Thanks." He took the tray, and then glanced round. "Get me about ten feet of deal slats today, will you – ask the shop to plane them down to an eighth of an inch."

"Yes, Dad," Matthew said, still subdued. He had probably been working too hard, Gideon decided, but there might be something else. Kate would know.

Gideon took the tea upstairs, and saw Priscilla disappearing into the bathroom, fair hair still in a net. When he went into his bedroom, Kate was beginning to sit up, and pushing her hair with her right hand; her hair net was on the bedside table. Kate first thing in the morning was something to see; she always looked as if sleep had not only thoroughly refreshed her, but had taken years off her age. Yet her hair was much greyer than he had noticed before, you couldn't fight your years. She was forty-nine, he was fifty-three. He put the tray on the foot of the bed, went across and closed the door, and then poured out.

"What's the secrecy about, dear?" Kate asked.

"Dunno," answered Gideon. "I wondered if young Matt had said anything to you about his troubles."

Kate looked startled.

"Troubles?"

"So he hasn't?"

"George, what has he been telling you?"

"Nothing," said Gideon, "but I thought he was on the verge of a confidence downstairs. How long has he been sleeping badly?"

"Ever since that examination," Kate answered slowly. "It didn't seem to worry him when he was swotting for it, but at the exam time and afterwards he seemed to be worried too much, he thought he was going to fail. He hasn't been really himself since, and I've an idea that it's worry about how he'll get on at Cambridge. He thinks he'll feel a little out of his depth, mixing with the sons of belted earls and—"

"Nonsense," interrupted Gideon flatly. "He might have a bit of an inferiority complex when he gets there, but it wouldn't get him down now. See if you can get something out of him, will you?"

"George, what do you suspect?"

"Dunno that I suspect anything," Gideon replied. "I've just got a feeling that he wanted to talk but couldn't bring himself to. Now don't you start worrying!"

"It can't be anything serious," Kate said hopefully.

When Gideon left, at a quarter to nine, and determined to be punctual at the office this morning, nothing else had been said about Matthew. They had all breakfasted together, Gideon felt replete, there had been no difficulty with the car, and Matthew had seen him out of the garage. He did not give a great deal of thought to the boy, but let his mind roam over the cases he knew would be up for briefing this morning, and speculation on what else had happened

during the night. Please God there hadn't been another fire.
Joe Bell had been in for some time, and the morning's
reports were on the desk. Gideon glanced through them,
relieved that Bell had not greeted him with bad news.

"Quiet night," Gideon remarked.

"We can do with one," said Bell. "Certainly there's nothing to write home about."

"Any messages?"

"No one's properly awake yet," Bell answered. "I've got
a feeling it's going to be a thin morning."

By a quarter to ten, he was proved right. Lemaitre,
Cornish, Margetson and Riddell all reported 'no progress'.
There was a ticklish little problem resulting from a raid on
a Mayfair house where gaming had long been suspected;
among the thirty detainees coming up for hearing this morning at Marlborough Street were three gentlemen who
claimed diplomatic privilege; already the fact that they had
been in a police cell for several hours was causing indignation and threats of reprisals.

"I'll check with the A.C.," Gideon said to the detective
inspector who had led the raid. "If I have my way they'll
claim their privilege from the dock. Okay, Pete." The C.I.
went out, and Gideon spent ten minutes reading the rest of
the reports. Even the telephone was more quiet than usual,
and he stood up suddenly.

"I'm going to have a quick tour this morning," he said.
"If I'm urgently wanted and don't answer the radio, try
KL and QR."

"Right, George," Bell said. "Not much of a morning for
a joy-ride, though."

"Could be worse," said Gideon.

Whenever he wanted a quick look round the Divisions, as
now, he drove himself. The rain was still coming down in
squalls and with the wind was whipping the surface of the
Thames to hissing fury. Traffic was noticeably thinner than
usual, which meant that the day-time motorists were staying
at home. Gideon drove over Westminster Bridge, and
within fifteen minutes was sliding to a standstill outside the
QR Divisional Headquarters. When he looked at the old

early Victorian building, he reflected that it could almost rate for demolition, there were far too many fire traps among the police stations. How right was Carmichael? He went in, finding policemen eager to salute, and doors opening as if at the wave of a wand. Manning was in his office. It wasn't surprising to find this scrupulously tidy, and looking as if the cleaners had only just left. Manning, big, plump, bald and smooth-shaven, held out his hand.

"Glad to see you, George. Sit down, and what about a cuppa?"

"Wouldn't mind that after I've had a look at Hilton Terrace, and this telephone kiosk," Gideon said. "Any news about Mrs. Jarvis yet?"

"A neighbour says she's getting on top of the situation already," Manning reported. "I'm going to see her myself today to make sure there's nothing she needs."

"Good," approved Gideon. "Mind if I go along to the scene of the Hilton Terrace fire?"

"Like me for a guide?"

"Can you spare the time?"

"Spare anything for the Big White Chief," said Manning. "As a matter of fact I was going to have another look round myself today some time. Margetson's over there with a couple of our chaps and a man from the Fire Service."

Except for the blackened, gutted buildings, a few barricades to make sure that no one could get too close to the wreckage, things were back to normal in Hilton Terrace. On the outside landings of the tenements which remained were lines of washing, and more washing hung from windows. Only a small, listless crowd watched the police and the fire assessors among the ruins. Gideon spent five minutes with them, finding out that Margetson still had nothing to report, and then went to the telephone kiosk. It was easy to see how right Margetson had been.

"Satisfied?" asked Manning.

"Always like to see for myself. Thanks," Gideon said. "Pity we haven't got some kind of a line on the man yet."

"We will, soon," Manning said.

*　　*　　*

As it happened the man whom Mrs. Tennison knew as Mr. Brown was within a fifteen minutes' walk of the two police chiefs at that moment. Sleeping. He had been out on night work at a big hotel again.

Gideon drove from Lambeth across the river at London Bridge to Bethnal Green, the scene of the first and fourth fires. There were practically no traces of either, for the other slum houses in the street were being pulled down. A few blackened rafters and, unexpectedly, the wreck of a burnt-out car in a plot of land opposite the scene of the first one were the only signs. He went from there to Canning Town, where the burnt-out tenements survived. They made a gaping blot on the district of row upon row of four-storey tenements, all of them fire traps, and each almost criminally overcrowded. Next, he drove to Whitechapel, and pulled up and looked at a new building going up near the burned hovels. Carmichael was right about one thing: the districts were all very much the same. They gave a sense of over-crowding, of squalor, of shameful slum conditions, in spite of the television antennae at practically every roof, in spite of the bright new furniture in the nearby shops, the gown and dress stores, the crammed food shops. There was a lot of money about, and comparatively little poverty in the old sense, but the trappings of poverty remained. A family with an income of thirty or forty pounds a week might still live in two rooms, sleeping three and four in a room, sexes mixed up far into the early teens. Here, crime spawned, sex knowledge came very early, life was vastly different from life in Hurlingham. Yet the women looked healthy, well made-up and well-dressed. Gideon saw a lad about Matthew's age cycling along and whistling, a small skull cap on the back of his head, school satchel flopping up and down on his back. Had Kate talked to Matthew yet? Gideon hardly gave that a thought, but drove back towards the City, and then cut across towards North London. When he reached the Angel, Islington, he pulled up alongside a policeman, and asked:

"How do I get to Littleton Street, please?"

"Straight along here, sir, first on the left, and then second on the right," the constable answered. "You can't miss it, there's a big warehouse on the corner – Debben's – general wholesaler's place. Turn sharp right there. You want to be careful turning the corner, the lorries and vans come out a bit fast sometimes."

"Thanks," said Gideon, and then saw recognition dawn in the man's eyes, followed by a look of astonishment. He drove on, pleased as always at the evidence of courteousness and helpfulness among the Force. These chaps today had a hell of a job, far worse than when he had been on the beat. For one thing, if he'd given a young idiot a clout, in his day, no one had complained. He saw the big ugly concrete building of Debben's, Wholesale Merchants, and as he turned the corner, a lorry swung out of the loading yard, and the driver jammed on his brakes. What made people behave as if saving seconds justified risking life?

Another van came out, more slowly. It was a big one. The driver was a burly man, in his shirtsleeves in spite of the coolness and the rain. He had thick hair which grew low on his forehead, and eyes buried beneath a matt of black eyebrows. Gideon thought: Not a customer I'd like the girls to meet in the dark, and then rebuked himself; the theory of Lombroso died hard even in the minds of men who had never really believed it. This chap was probably a model father and husband. He waved Gideon on, and Gideon did not see the way he looked towards the house where Ivy Manson had been attacked.

John Stewart Briggs did not know that the car he waved to was driven by a man from Scotland Yard. He was simply on his best behaviour, because he did not want the slightest trouble with the police. There was one good thing: no one had questioned him, and no one seemed to suspect that he had sometimes given the Manson kid a ride.

Carson of KL was waiting for Gideon. He was a short, dapper man, with a pale face, well-dressed, well-groomed, somehow giving an impression of being cold-blooded. No one at the Yard knew him well. He was a good, painstaking and conscientious policeman, and a better detective than most – and he was the most formal man on the Force.

"Good morning, Commander," he greeted.

"'Morning, Carson."

"I regret to inform you that we have as yet obtained no useful information," announced Carson.

"Pity. How're the parents?"

"There appears to be a real possibility that the mother will have to go into hospital," Carson deposed. "She is showing signs of shock and acute mental distress, and I understand that her husband, relations and a neighbour have not been able to make her utter a word for the past eighteen hours. The child came very late, the woman was forty-five at the time of birth, and both parents idolised her." The way Carson reported this made the facts seem even more hideous; his very coldness made them speak for themselves. "A doctor is with her now, and at my suggestion is arranging for a consultation shortly with a specialist."

"Hmm," grunted Gideon. "And you haven't picked up a thing?"

"Not yet," said Carson. "There is one approach which I have not yet made, because it seemed to me that we might be wise to hold our hand for a short while."

Gideon forebore to say: "Supposing the killer does it again?"

"It would be most unusual if the man were to make another attack so quickly upon the first," went on Carson, "and I do not believe there is any danger in delay." Gideon smothered a grin at himself. "The place I have in mind is Debben's Warehouse," went on Carson unemotionally. "I am told that it is the custom of some of the drivers to give the children of the district a ride from time to time. That does not often happen, and is expressly forbidden by the company, but on wet days and out of the kindness of their hearts the drivers occasionally ignore this company by-law. I propose to wait until this evening, and then to have every driver questioned in his own home. If I were to go to the warehouse and accost each man as he returns from a journey, I think it might alarm anyone who is guilty, and give him a chance to cover up. As it is, one of the men may have seen the dead child with a man, even if none of them is involved."

"Good thought," Gideon approved. "How many drivers are there?"

"Eleven. And they know the district thoroughly."

"Need any more help?" asked Gideon.

"I think the Division now has sufficient men," Carson said. "Thank you, all the same." He glanced along the mean little street, and saw a black Rover car turn the corner. "I think this will be the medical consultant, Dr. Forbeson."

"Let me know what he says," Gideon said. "I'll get going." He didn't add: "There's obviously no need for me here," but he felt very warm towards Carson. Passing the warehouse, he glanced in at several vans at the loading platform. If the killer were there, then he had been driving in and out of this yard for a long time with lust and desire and evil in his mind. In some ways, this emphasised the worst feature in Gideon's life: the knowledge that as he drove about London, as he walked, as he sat in his office, as he talked with Kate, whatever he was doing and whenever he was doing it, people were living their everyday lives, most of them with no thought of evil, but others planning every kind of crime and beastliness.

Another firebug, perhaps; another killer of policemen; another company fraud. He often reminded himself that it was all going on at this very moment. Crimes were being born, hopes were being raised, people had the mark of Cain on them, others had the drab mark of prison uniforms. It was an inescapable fact that this London through which he was driving, and of which he was part, was a spawning ground of crime, and people yet unborn would one day kill or maim or steal or cheat. Occasionally this realisation gave Gideon a sense of gloomy hopelessness, born out of the vast homogeneous mass of people and the impossibility of seeing into their minds. But there was another side, the good side.

Ninety-nine men out of a hundred would no more think of crime than of beating their own wives or children. And these van drivers, for instance, noticed a great deal that went on – there was nearly always a witness to be found if the police probed deeply enough.

On the other side of London, Clapper's wife slipped the policeman who was following her, and went to meet the man who had worked with her husband on the bank job. She met him where they had met before, in a quiet cul-de-sac not far from the docks, with a high blank wall on one side, a lower wall of an old disused timber yard on the other. He was waiting, a man of medium height, thin, with dark, rather shadowy eyes.

"What's on your mind, Bee?" he asked at once.

Beatrice Clapper said clearly:

"You told me you would see that Lenny didn't get into any trouble. Remember that?"

"Now be sensible, Bee," the man protested. "I didn't put Lenny away, you know that as well as I do. He'll only get a couple of years, even if he's found guilty, and I'll hire a good lawyer who may get him off altogether. He'll be looked after, anyhow, and so will you. There's no need to get worked up."

Almost before he had finished, the woman said flatly:

"You're not going to talk your way out of this one. Either you get Lenny out quick, or I'll tell the police you were with him. And it's no use trying to hide out in Brighton, either."

"Who told you I had a place at Brighton?" the man demanded. "I never told Lenny."

"You've never told Lenny enough," Bee Clapper retorted, and gave a satisfied laugh. "As a matter of fact Lenny doesn't know I know. I was down in Brighton for a day's outing this spring, and I saw you all dolled up to the nines. Mr. *Simpson*, isn't it?"

Obviously she felt quite sure she had the man cornered, as she went on: "Lenny's not going to stand the rap for you or anyone. I'm not joking, either."

"No," said the man, slowly. "I can see you're not." He stared at her for a moment, then seemed to explode into movement. He shot out his left hand, slapped it over Beatrice Clapper's mouth and thrust her head back. Her teeth slid over the palm of his hand.

She did not even see the knife as it flashed towards her throat.

Gideon reached the Yard a little after one o'clock. He had a quick but substantial meal in the canteen, and went up to his office, where Bell was relieved by a younger man during his lunch hour.

"Anything in, Parsons?" Gideon asked.

"Nothing much, sir."

"What happened over at Marlborough Street?"

"I'm told that those chaps didn't claim diplomatic immunity after all, sir – they were each fined fifty pounds. The owner of the house was remanded on bail of a thousand pounds for a week, sir."

"Sounds about right," said Gideon. "All right, you carry on." He picked up reports, and began to make notes recommending courses of action, and he read everything that had come in since he had last been in the office, so that when the time came to discuss the particular job he would know what he was talking about. He read with intensive concentration for half an hour, barely nodding to Bell when he came in, but glad that Bell was here to answer the telephone. It was three o'clock when one of his own phones rang.

"Gideon," Gideon said, dropping his pencil, stretching himself, and not troubling to stifle a yawn.

"Mr. Cornish would like a word —"

"Put him through."

"Yes, sir." There was hardly a pause before Cornish came on the line, and on the instant Gideon could tell that he was excited. "George, Clapper's wife had her throat cut," Cornish blurted out.

Even to Gideon, so used to the unexpected, this was a shock out of the blue. It took him several seconds to adjust himself, to picture that brassy-mannered, hard-voiced woman with the flamboyant make-up and the brazen manner – and, he recalled with horrid vividness, a slender, smooth white throat.

"You there, George?" Cornish asked.

"Yes," Gideon said at last. "Where is she?"

"We were watching her, had a D.O. on her tail, but she shook him off at Aldgate Station," Cornish answered. "That was just before lunch. Two kids found her body in a yard they play in, in Whitechapel. I've just seen her. As far as I can tell she was killed in a cul-de-sac and her body was lifted up to the wall and dropped over. I've got the Division alerted, and if you'll fix a general request for information about her —"

"Yes," Gideon said. "I'll get Clapper in from Brixton, too. Had photographs taken?"

"Yes."

"I want a print as soon as I can get it," said Gideon. "Keep in touch." He rang off, and called across to Bell in the same breath: "Call all Central Divisions to report the movements of Mrs. Lenny – Beatrice Eliza – Clapper. You've got her age and description. Make it urgent. She's had her throat cut."

"Gawd!"

"Ask Brixton to bring Clapper over here. If they prefer it, we'll send a couple of men over to pick him up."

"Right."

"What's holding you back?" demanded Gideon. He pushed his hair off his forehead and Bell lifted the receiver, and for a moment he felt almost sick. She may have been brassy, bold and brazen, but she had been a handsome, vital woman, and had been standing in front of this desk only last evening. While he had been driving about London, she had been having her throat cut. One slash – and the vitality was gone for ever. That wasn't really the worst – there were the indications that her murderer was the man who had killed the man at Bournemouth, six months ago. Cornish had been right to be edgy about him. But after this they shouldn't be long finding out who it was. Should they?

* * *

Clapper was a big, lean-hipped, over-dressed man, just about a match for his wife, good-looking in a bold way and with a flamboyant air, but less sure of himself than he looked. He stood in front of Gideon's desk just twenty-three hours after his wife had, and he had no idea what had happened.

"Now when are you going to tell us who worked with you on the bank tunnelling job?" Gideon asked mildly.

"Why don't you stop wasting your time?" sneered Clapper.

"Frightened in case he gets you if you talk?"

"No one scares *me*, Gee-Gee."

"Anyone scare your wife?" inquired Gideon. He felt no compassion at all for this man, who must know just what kind of criminal he was protecting.

"You keep my wife out of this, Gee-Gee," Clapper said sharply.

"I would have," Gideon said. "We all would have. Your friend decided not to." He turned a photograph of Mrs. Clapper over so that Clapper, looking down, could see it; and it was not a pretty sight below the chin.

Clapper stared at the photograph without a change of expression for at least half a minute. Gideon watched him closely. The colour drained from his face. His eyes, bright and impudent, gradually became shadowed. His lips parted, until he began to breathe through his mouth, and every breath seemed to become harsher.

"Is that what you protected your friend for?" demanded Gideon. "So that he could do that?"

He wasn't prepared for what followed. Clapper gave a rasping, choking breath, and collapsed. He struck his chin on the edge of Gideon's desk as he fell, and was unconscious in front of the desk before Gideon or Bell could move.

CHAPTER VIII

POLICE MESSAGE

JOE BELL's bald patch met Gideon as he rounded the desk; for an elderly man, Joe had moved fast. Now he was feeling Clapper's pulse, while straightening out the big, handsome body. Clapper's mouth was slack, his eyes were slightly open and had a glazed look, his whole body was slack.

"Hell of a crack he caught himself, but he's all right," Bell said. He took his hand away. "Want a nurse up?"

"Yes," Gideon said. "He's going to have a nasty bruise on that chin, and before we're through he'll be saying we hit him. Leave him as he is." Bell moved to his desk and telephone, and Gideon bent down and picked up the photograph of Clapper' wife, which the man had knocked to the floor. He still felt no compassion, but was a little uneasy; he had probably done the wrong thing, and if he had, this could develop into one of the awkward cases. Clapper's solicitor, who had already seen the accused twice, was a little-known man named Lewisham, and although Gideon hadn't seen him, he had been told that he was very shrewd. A complaint to the Press that a man had been man-handled at the Yard was always liable to work up a newspaper wave of public 'indignation', and everyone who wanted to catch the Yard on the wrong foot would exert himself to feed the fire.

"He'll talk, after this," Bell said, and obviously he didn't take the third degree possibility very seriously. He might be right not to. Gideon sat on the corner of his desk, while waiting, and ran through everything which had led up to this moment. A murdered night-watchman in Bournemouth; the bank job after a tunnelling; Clapper's capture; Clapper's silence; his wife's insolence and confidence. They had both been so positive that the man or men they refused to name would look after them.

Clapper began to stir as the door opened to admit a male nurse, one of the two always on duty in the first aid room at the Yard. Expertly, he lifted Clapper to a chair, checked his pulse, raised his eyelids with a practised thumb, and said:

"Nothing to worry about here, sir." He felt the jaw, already puffy and pink where it had struck the desk. "Nothing damaged." He glanced at Gideon's right fist, and then asked: "How did it happen, sir?"

"He banged his chin on the desk when I told him his wife had been murdered," Gideon answered, and held out his hands. "No damaged knuckles, Smith!"

"Oh, that didn't occur to me, sir."

"Didn't it?" asked Gideon dryly. "Well, what do you recommend?"

"A nip wouldn't do him any harm, and after that some hot sweet tea and coffee."

"I'll fix the nip, you fix the hot drink," Gideon ordered, and the nurse gave the impression that he was glad to hurry out.

Gideon saw Bell with a brandy flask in his hand, and nodded. Bell put the mouthpiece to Clapper's lips, Clapper gulped, gasped, began to turn his head and to open his eyes. He looked straight at Gideon, who saw the momentary gleam of intelligence in those brown eyes, then saw them glaze over; that was enough to tell him that Clapper was going to play for time.

"Come on, Clapper," Gideon said heavily. "You're not fooling us. Who's the man you're sheltering?"

Clapper's eyes remained stubbornly closed.

"Let's have it," Gideon went on, and he felt his fists bunching, felt more like striking the man than he had before. It was impossible to say why, but this incident seemed to him to be really menacing; some kind of sixth sense of anxiety was building up in him. "He murdered your wife, Clapper. Who is he?"

Clapper still pretended to be unconscious.

Gideon turned round, picked up an ebony ruler from his desk, and brought it down sharply on the edge of the desk. It made a crack like a pistol shot, and Clapper started up, his eyes opening wide and scared. Gideon slid the ruler up his sleeve, Bell smothered a grin, and Gideon went on:

"You might as well tell us. We'll get him for the murder of the Bournemouth night-watchman, and of your wife. He hasn't a chance. And you needn't think you'll be safe if you continue to cover him. That's the mistake your wife made."

Clapper moistened his lips, but said nothing.

"You won't help yourself whatever you do," Gideon went on, and again he felt his anger rising. "You might be able to avenge your wife, though. Don't you realise what happened? She went to see this precious pal of yours. She wouldn't talk to us, she wouldn't do anything to put him in trouble, but he cut her throat. Does that make him worth protecting?"

Clapper muttered: "I want to see my lawyer. I've got a right, I want to see my lawyer." He put up his right hand to the left side of his jaw, touched the bruise gingerly, and winced. "I'm not saying anything, you might as well save your breath."

He was still silent when the nurse brought in hot tea. He was silent when Cornish arrived, and when they took him back to Brixton.

"You know the truth about him, don't you?" Cornish said to Gideon and Bell. "He's more scared than he ever was. He was frightened to talk before, and now he sees what's happened to his wife, he feels as if his throat might be cut next."

Gideon didn't speak.

"Looks like it," Bell said.

Gideon grunted. "Could be. Cornish, you've got a bigger job than ever on your hands. This was in NE Division. Go over and see Hopkinson, and keep right on to this job. You can have any help you want, just ask me or Joe. All clear?"

"Yes," said Cornish. "Know what I think we ought to do, George?"

"What?"

"Make a house-to-house visit around the spot where the body was found. There aren't many men who'd fail to notice Bee Clapper. Then we ought to have a radio and TV appeal for anyone who saw her from the time she left Aldgate Station this morning. I know it isn't easy to fix the television people, but—"

"I'll fix it," Gideon promised. "What we've got on this job is a man who'll kill anybody to save himself. You get cracking."

Before Cornish was out of the office, Gideon was asking for the Assistant Commissioner, who would have to authorise the appeal to the British Broadcasting Corporation and the London Independent Television network.

Among those who saw the newscasts which threw a picture of Beatrice Clapper on to the television screens of London and the Home Counties, was mild-mannered little Mr. 'Brown'. He was not going to work tonight, he had told Mrs. Tennison, so he would see a little television, and then go upstairs to his room and read.

John Stewart Briggs saw it, too.

For the murderer of Ivy Manson, it was a very bad half hour. He was home a little after six o'clock, and his sister was sitting in front of the television screen, knitting in her hands, table laid for their supper. Briggs went into the scullery, to wash under the tap, and was drying his hands when he heard the announcer say:

". . . And now we have an urgent police message, about the murder of . . ."

Briggs felt as if someone had stabbed him. He was in the doorway, towel still in his hands, and his sister was so startled that she gaped at him instead of the screen.

". . . and any persons who saw this woman in the vicinity of Aldgate Tube Station and Whitechapel between one o'clock and two thirty this afternoon is asked to communicate with the nearest police station, or with Scotland Yard, telephone number Whitehall 1212."

Briggs swung away.

His sister said nothing, just stared at his back, then got

up and went to the oven, where a fish pie was baking. She took it out with an oven cloth, muttering when a spot of the milk spilled on to her calloused thumb. She put the enamel dish on to the table, called: "Come and get it," and was about to serve the pie when there was a sharp rat-tat at the front door.

"Oh, blast them," she muttered. "Go and see who the hell that is, Jack."

"Go yourself," Briggs retorted roughly.

"Do you want your supper or —"

"I'll serve. You see who it is."

His sister stared at him, frowning, then turned slowly away. She had never known him in such a peculiar mood. She went to the front door, so broad and fat that her hips touched each side of the narrow passage, she was just a mass of flabby flesh. As she opened the door, she sensed that her brother was watching and listening.

Two men stood outside, both big fellows, and she felt quite sure that these were detectives.

"Is Mr. John Stewart Briggs at home, please?" the larger of the two asked.

"Who – who wants him?"

"We are police officers," the man went on, and held out a card. "We are making inquiries into the murder of Ivy Manson, and we would like to talk to Mr. Briggs."

"He – he might be in," the sister said, uneasily. "I'll go and see, he usually comes in the back way." She pushed the door to, but the man's foot was against it, and it would not close. She turned round, and saw the kitchen door shut. She leaned against the wall, shocked and almost overcome, then heard footsteps behind her. A man tried to squeeze past, but her great bulk blocked the way, and her sixteen stones could not easily be moved. "Wh – what do you think you're playing at?" she managed to mutter. "Wha —"

The man pushed past, reached the kitchen door, and tried to thrust it open; but it was locked. "Back way!" he bellowed, and the other man swung round and raced towards a corner and an alley which led to the back of these houses. He put his shoulder against the kitchen door, and at

the second onslaught it crashed in. The scullery door and
the door leading to the tiny backyard were open, and the
detective jumped forward, failed to see the chair upturned
in the doorway, and crashed into it. He did not see or hear
Briggs; nor did the other man. But within five minutes a
radio message was flashed to the Yard, and the general call
was out in the next few minutes.

After Pamela Harrison had watched the police appeal
and the picture of Beatrice Clapper, she picked up a fashion
magazine and began to look at pictures of beautifully dressed
and perfectly made-up women, thinking as she so often did
that there must *be* a way to hold Tony. . . .

Her head ached, and she went to the bathroom to get
some aspirins. Then she studied the magazine, wondering
what would be the surest way. A new make-up, perhaps a
new hair-style, certainly some new clothes. She could afford
all this now that the children were away, and anything was
worth trying.

Her husband and Chloe Duval, however, did not see the
newscast of the police message. They were on the bed in
Chloe's little flat, while the trailing policeman sat in a small
private car, reading a newspaper. He was within sight of
the house and of Harrison's trade car, this time a Vauxhall,
and his instructions were to do nothing except follow Harrison, unless the man took his girl friend to a secluded spot.

It wasn't until the orgasm was over, and the mood
changed, that Harrison began to think of that 'suicide'
again. Pam was always taking aspirins for her headaches,
and she also had some sleeping pills. There must be a way
to give her an overdose, without anyone dreaming she hadn't
taken it herself.

The Jarvis family saw the appeal, too – Neil, while playing with a clockwork motor car which a neighbour had
given him, the younger girl while looking through a new
comic book, also a gift, Hester as she laid the table for
supper, her mother casually while she cut bread-and-butter.

Jarvis had never liked ready-cut bread, he had always said that it lacked real body.

Charles and Joan Ericson and Jimmy Roscoe saw the programme at the house in Esher, during a curious kind of impasse in their discussions. Jimmy had come back from his hiding place in Kent, and as far as he knew, the police had not yet seen him. He was a short, plump man with curly fair hair and a ready smile; until this time of crisis, Joan Ericson had never known him anything but bright and breezy, a little superficial in his amiability, much more popular with Michael and Joanna when they had been younger, for instance, than he was now; the children seemed to have seen through the falseness of much of his gaiety to his rather shallow personality.

He was opposed to making any statement to the police, and in favour of trying to get out of the country. The struggle was going to be between him and Joan, Ericson knew; at last he began to realise that his wife was his strength.

Among the millions of others who saw Beatrice Clapper's photograph on the television screen was a man who knew her and Lenny Clapper well. His name was Scarfe – Alan Paul Scarfe, known to his friends and intimates as Scar, partly because of the coincidence of the ugly scar at the back of his left hand. Those who had known him for a long time knew that he had saved his life with that scar; he had been set upon, fifteen years ago, by two men whom he had cheated out of card winnings, and they would have sliced him up. He had flung his left hand up in front of his face, to take the worst of the slash, and before anything worse had happened, friends had come to his rescue. But he had not wanted to go to the nearest doctor, who might have let something out to the police. Alan Paul Scarfe had trusted nobody but himself even in those days. So he had been patched up by a drunken ex-doctor who had been struck off the Medical Register for illegal abortions. The stitches had been badly placed, and the wounded hand never healed smoothly; a kind of ridge, like a piece of knotted string, ran from the middle of his hand near the knuckle right up to the wrist and out of sight beneath the shirt cuff.

So Scarfe wore gloves whenever he could.

He had always been a fancy dresser, and these days he went to one of the best as well as one of the most expensive tailors in the East End. His shirt cuffs always showed up spotlessly, just half an inch beneath the sleeves. His tie, breast pocket handkerchief and socks always matched. He wore good quality cuff-links and a gold tie-pin with just a little pattern of diamond in it. Almost the only thing which did not carry his monogram was his flick-knife, with its razor sharp blade. He had sterilised that blade after returning from the meeting with Bee Clapper, and now there was not the slightest risk of her blood being found on it.

He had two other identities.

As Alan Peter Spender he had a small apartment in a Mayfair street leading to Berkeley Square. In Brighton, he had a flat under the name of Simpson. He was known in the Mayfair neighbourhood as a man who kept himself very much to himself, but was generous with tradespeople and courteous whenever he met neighbours. They had no reason even to dream that whenever it suited him he could put on on old suit, a cloth cap and a choker, change his voice, and become a 'typical' Cockney.

He had been the brains behind the old Bournemouth robbery, and had killed the night watchman. His methods had been so different every time he did a job that the police had not 'typed' him. It had never occurred to him that the small darn in the right thumb of his glove might one day be used in evidence against him. Those gloves fitted almost like a second skin, and were invaluable, enabling him to have complete freedom of finger movement, without leaving prints on a job.

He had planned and carried out over a dozen robberies during the past seven years, and now had a fortune of over a hundred thousand pounds stored away in five different banks in London, one in Paris, one in Milan, and another in New York.

Very few people knew him both as Scar – or Alan Paul Scarfe – and as Alan Peter Spender. No one knew him under all three names; the Clappers were among the four people who knew him as Scarfe and Spender.

After Clapper's arrest, Scarfe had been uneasy, but had no reason to believe that Clapper would name him as Spender. He had always paid Clapper well, and the man knew that he would be looked after when he came out of prison, and that his wife would live in comfort while Clapper was away. But Bee Clapper had made him realise that it wasn't going to be so straight-forward; that had been obvious when she had telephoned him at the Mayfair flat, demanding to see him urgently. Scarfe had weighed up the situation carefully. Bee Clapper was a highly strung and emotional woman, and the only way to make sure she didn't give him away to the police would be to kill her. But if he did, Clapper might break down, and give his second identity away.

So there was a grave risk, either way, but Clapper could only give his second, London, identity away; Bee could destroy his third and last hide-out.

So, he had had to kill her.

He knew Clapper very well, however, and believed that when the man heard about his wife's murder, his first reaction would be one of fear for himself – fear of what would happen after he was released from prison. There was an even chance that Clapper would keep his mouth shut.

Until he knew for certain how Clapper would react to Bee's murder, Scarfe *alias* Spender knew that he would have to fall back on his third line of defence, the third identity – of Arthur Philip Simpson of Brighton. Instead of going back to the Mayfair flat, he took everything that could give away his real identity to Brighton that afternoon. If Clapper kept quiet, he could pick up his other identities as it suited him.

He had a small flat overlooking the sea on the east side of the promenade, in front of the miniature railway, well away from the gaudy, garish shops and catch-pennies on the pier and the front on the other side. No smell of fried fish, candy-floss or rock, no reeling, rolling crowds wearing silly hats and singing silly songs, passed here.

Week-end flats were common enough in Brighton, no one was ever surprised that Simpson occupied the flat only at week-ends, and for a week now and again. It was small and self-contained, and no one ever worried about the fact that his week-end companions were often different – certainly he had a variety of mistresses each summer.

He was sitting with his back to the window, oblivious of the gentle hiss of the sea running back across the smooth pebbles, watching the television screen and half expecting a police message. When it came, he tightened his lips and watched and listened carefully. Once it was over, he went and switched off, smiling thinly.

As Arthur Philip Simpson, he would stay in Brighton and await developments.

There was no reason at all why it should be known to him that only a few minutes' walk away from his flat, in a house which had been converted into flatlets of convenience, a girl named Chloe Duval had recently moved. Nor could he know that Anthony Harrison, cold-blooded murderer of three women, was in that flat at this very moment; or that at the request of the Sussex and the Brighton police a Scotland Yard detective sergeant was sitting and watching nearby.

Gideon saw the photograph of Bee Clapper on his own television screen, chiefly to satisfy himself that everything had been carried out as he had hoped. Kate was upstairs. He had come home earlier than usual and she had been in the middle of a bath. None of the children was in. He found himself thinking of Matthew, and wondering whether Kate had got anything out of their boy, and wondering how long she would be. He went into the kitchen and opened the larder door, pondered, cut a piece off a hunk of cheese, and took an apple out of a dish on the dresser, and munching first one and then the other, stood looking at the neat little back garden. The water was gushing out of the waste, so

Kate wouldn't be long. He heard her moving about, and at twenty-five past six, she came hurrying downstairs. He saw at once that she had something on her mind, she even looked anxious and worried, and that gave him a shock.

"Hallo, Kate," he greeted, and gulped down a piece of apple. "Catch you bending?"

"I didn't expect you quite so early," she admitted. "It's silly to have a bath when the house is empty, someone always calls. What kind of a day have you had, dear?" The question was perfunctory, whereas usually she made him feel as if she really wanted to know.

"What's up, Kate?" he asked. "Is Matthew really in trouble?"

"Yes," she answered.

Then the telephone bell rang, and it seemed like a knife slicing the atmosphere between them. It was no use ignoring it. Gideon muttered, "Blurry thing!" explosively, and leaned across the kitchen table to pick up the extension instrument. 'Blurry for bloody', adopted when he had found the children mimicking his 'bloody', would never leave him now. "Gideon," he announced harshly.

Kate saw the tightening of his grip on the telephone. She sensed the way his thoughts were wrenched off what she had said. She moved past him, doing up a button at the back of her blouse; she was always inclined to prefer separates.

Gideon said: "How serious?"

He paused.

"I'll come as soon as I can," he said, and put the receiver down. He turned and looked at Kate, raising his hands in a curiously appealing little gesture – and as he did so, he realised that a crisis had developed in this last few seconds. Kate had come hurrying, anxious to tell him about Matthew's trouble, and God knew he wanted to share it with her. It wasn't often, these days, that there was any serious conflict between home interests and the Yard's, but in the past they had sometimes clashed dangerously. He had sworn he would never let anything come between him and Kate again.

She was looking out of the window.

"What is it?"

Gideon answered: "They've cornered the man who killed Ivy Manson. He's shut himself up in a warehouse yard, and he's at the wheel of a truck containing a lot of paint. He says he'll set the paint on fire and drive it at our chaps and the firemen in front of it if they don't let him pass." Gideon stopped and saw the expression change in Kate's eyes, knew that the fact that this was Ivy Manson's killer had caused the change. He sensed the struggle going on within her. The fact that it was such a struggle made the situation worse: what the devil was the trouble with Matthew? What could the lad have done which would worry her so much?

"Why don't you come with me?" he asked suddenly. "We can talk on the way. It'll take half an hour at least to get there."

Her face lit up.

"I haven't put the car away yet," Gideon went on. "I'd thought we might go for a spin. Five minutes?"

"Less," Kate promised, and as she passed him to go upstairs, she brushed his cheek lightly with her fingers. "Bless you." She hurried upstairs, and Gideon strode across to the larder again, cut off a larger piece of cheese and put it into a tin half full of biscuits, dropped some apples into his capacious coat pocket, and was at the foot of the stairs when Kate came hurrying down, legs and ankles slim and trim for so tall and fine-bodied a woman, wearing a cloth coat trimmed at the collar and cuffs with mink. He handed her the cheese, biscuits and apples.

"We can start on these, and if the Islington job doesn't take too long we'll have a meal up Town somewhere." He opened the passenger door for her, slammed it, and went round to his own seat. As he drove off along the quiet street, passing the parked cars of neighbours, he wished that it had been possible to talk to Kate about Matthew quietly and at home; but better this way than not at all.

"Well," he demanded, "what's the bother?"

"You're not going to like it," Kate said, quietly. "Matthew has got a girl into trouble."

CHAPTER IX

TROUBLE

THEY had just turned a corner which led towards one of the main thoroughfares, New King's Road, and there was only a cyclist on the move. Gideon glanced swiftly at Kate, his expression showing how startled he was, and for that second he had no reaction but of shock. He was not even in complete control of the car, and it swerved towards the cyclist. He straightened out quickly, said: "Sorry," and stared straight ahead. He knew that Kate was studying him, and guessing what was going on in his mind; the confusion and the astonishment. Matthew, of all people; he wasn't yet nineteen years old, he was on his way to Cambridge, he had such great hopes – the bloody young fool.

He didn't say that to Kate, but turned into New King's Road. There wasn't a great deal of traffic, all except the sweetshops, the pubs and the newsagents' shops were closed.

"I suppose there's no doubt about it," Gideon said at last.

"I don't think so, George."

"Couldn't be some little bitch taking him for a ride?"

Kate didn't answer.

"Could that be it" asked Gideon, and his hopes lifted.

"No," said Kate.

She would not be so definite unless she was absolutely positive. Gideon glanced at her again, and saw that she was staring straight ahead. There was no sign of any emotional upset, but her eyes were very bright.

"Do you know the girl?"

"It's Helen Miall," Kate answered.

"Oh, God," breathed Gideon.

The Mialls were neighbours, and lived only five doors away from the Gideons. The children – two Mialls, and the middle three of the Gideon family – had gone to the same schools and the same Sunday schools, played the same games, attended the same parties. Helen Miall was nearly as familiar to Gideon as one of his own daughters in all but those little touches of family intimacy. She was rather a small, rather a shy girl, just a year older than Matthew; their birthdays usually fell in the same week, and in childhood there had often been a two-family celebration. She was a nice kid, too. Miall was an insurance agent who did fairly well, but his wife lacked Kate's taste in the home and Kate's careful use of money. They were pleasant and acceptable as neighbours, but there was one big obstacle to real friendship; they were strict chapel people, members of a small nonconformist group. There was nothing hypocritical about them; as far as Gideon knew they believed everything they said and did, but very few could have narrower religious views.

Kate began to talk more freely.

"Matt says they've been afraid of it for the past month, but she's two months late, and she's beginning to feel sick in the mornings. She's terrified of what her father and mother will say and do. And Matthew wasn't exactly anxious to talk to us."

"How did you get it out of him?"

"I could see that he was jumpy this morning, and you'd been so sure that he was worried, so I came straight out with it as soon as the others had gone off this morning," answered Kate. "I'd wondered if there was a girl – wondered if he'd fallen in love, or thought he had, and was beginning to wish he hadn't got to go to Cambridge. So I asked him if it was a girl. Then it just came out."

Gideon put out his left hand, and took Kate's.

"Nice work," he said.

"We talked about nothing else all the morning, of course," Kate said. "He's gone out until ten o'clock, now, I told him that I'd have told you by then. We must be back by ten, George."

"We will be." They were going over the bridge by St. Mark's College, and a train chugged underneath them. Gideon had completely forgotten John Stewart Briggs, and

the 'must be back by ten' had reminded him; but this time
the picture of Ivy Manson did not become very vivid. He
was thinking, among other things, that Matthew hadn't
dared to tell him and Kate earlier. A month ago it might
have been comparatively easy to help, but two clear months
gone made it difficult. Impossible, he told himself. What
had he been doing, to let the lad lose his head so? And why
hadn't Matt confided earlier? Was he, the father, an ogre?
Was Kate —

"He says that he couldn't bring himself to tell us until
they were sure, he didn't want to hurt us," Kate said. "I
think he's been tormented for the past month."

"No wonder he couldn't sleep or concentrate," said
Gideon gruffly. "Good job he'd got through his exams, this
would have put paid to any scholarship. Say anything about
marrying the girl?"

Kate said, very hesitantly: "Yes."

"What's he say?"

"He doesn't want to."

Gideon didn't speak.

"And nor does Helen," Kate went on.

"What the hell have they been up to, if they feel like that
about each other?" growled Gideon. "Goddammit, they're
old enough to know what they're doing. If they were talking about being hopelessly in love I could understand it,
but —"

He broke off, and Kate glanced at him but made no comment. He was forced to slow down near some traffic lights,
and then to stop. He turned to look at her, and for the first
time since they had got into the car, he grinned, and actually
chuckled.

"You see what an upright Victorian parent I am. Matt
probably knows me better than I know myself. Did he try
to explain?"

"Yes," answered Kate, and there was a warm note in her
voice, as if she were anxious to comfort him. Or Matthew?
"He hasn't talked to me like it for years – in fact he's never
talked to me like it, he was always shy about me bathing
him sooner than the others! Malcolm still couldn't care

less." Unexpectedly, she laughed, too, and the warm note was still in her voice. "There were three or four occasions."

"Good God!" gasped Gideon. "And that's funny."

"It's not funny in that way," Kate said, with the humour still deep in her voice, "but the way he broke *all* the bridges once he started confiding in me was rather – well, funny!" She gave the little laugh again. "George, can you remember when you were eighteen?"

"No."

"It won't help us if you and I get prudish or heavy-handed," Kate reasoned, suddenly changing her mood and tone. "When he first told me, I felt as if he'd committed the biggest crime in the calendar, but now —"

"Just tell me how he softened you into accepting three or four occasions, as you put it," Gideon growled.

"George," said Kate, and paused as if she meant to pick every word with great care, "it began at New Year's Eve, after the dance they went to at the tennis club. Do you remember Matt coming home almost tipsy? I wanted to send him up to bed, and you told me that he had to get broken in sooner or later, and if we let him get away with it his headache next morning would do more good than all the lectures."

"Kate," said Gideon, heavily. "I think you're trying to get me out on a limb. There's a world of difference between —"

"That was the first night," interrupted Kate. "The Mialls were out at Watch Night Service, but they'd allowed Helen to go to the dance. I was surprised at the time, I hadn't thought they would. Their house was empty, Helen had had drink for the first time in her life, and —"

"Oh, once I can understand."

"Matt says that it simply went to their heads," Kate interrupted. "From what I can gather, the – the experience was wonderful. For about a week, they were infatuated. Then they had a quarrel, and tried to avoid each other. Matt says they both felt a bit scared and rather ashamed. It was about a month before they saw each other except when they chanced to meet in the street. But when she missed her first month, Helen told him. If Matt's telling the truth, and I think he is, they both feel certain that they aren't in love and hate the thought of having to marry. That's worrying them more than anything else, I think. They're afraid that the Mialls and the Gideons will try to make them."

Gideon didn't respond for some time. He was driving much faster, and going along streets of tall terraced houses in a district which Kate hardly knew. In ten minutes they would be at the warehouse he had seen that afternoon; in ten minutes he had to switch from one nightmare to one of a different kind.

Nightmare.

"Blurry young pup," he said. "I know what I'd do with him."

"George —"

"I'd hand him over to Ted Miall for a week," Gideon growled, and Kate laughed, but this time there was a note of suppressed emotion in her voice.

"I know what you mean," she said. "What do you think Ted will say?"

"He'll throw the Bible at me, and every interpretation he, his minister and his wife have ever put into it. Oh, Lord, what a thing to happen." Gideon paused, for breath. "It's a hell of a situation, Kate. What ought we to do? Be really Victorian, or —" he broke off.

"Do you think the Mialls will try to insist on them getting married right away?"

"Don't know," said Gideon, and did not speak again until they were at the lights where he had spoken to the policeman that morning. He put a hand on Kate's knee, squeezed, and went on: "I'll go round and see Ted Miall as soon as we've talked to Matt. And I do *not* need telling that it won't do any good to go off the deep end with the boy."

The lights changed.

As he drove on, another kind of nightmare only just round the corner, he felt a little desperate, almost despairing. He could almost picture his son and Helen, a little slip of a thing – and then he remembered that the last time he had

seen her, she had seemed to have matured suddenly; instead
of a gentle curve at the bosom she had been provocatively
bra'd. The picture of them fumbling, excited, eager, tipsy,
glowing, the picture of them locked together, was strangely
and almost painfully vivid. If they wanted to marry, it
wouldn't be so bad, but bad enough.

There was another aspect which he hadn't yet thought
about, but would have to : what would be best for Matthew
and the girl, apart from what they ought to do judged by
orthodox moral standards? And what would be best for
them, apart from their present mood of antipathy towards
one another? Suddenly he had been jolted out of a kind of
smug satisfaction with his own family into a position of acute
difficulty.

The essential thing was to have time to think clearly;
nothing must be done in haste, whatever Ted Miall wanted.

The brief mood of rationalising vanished in a sudden
burst of anger.

Of all the things to happen! Matthew and a girl he'd
known all his life, friends, neighbours. It couldn't be worse.
It couldn't —

Then he saw a police car drawn up at the corner which
led to Debben's Warehouse, and noticed the reflected glare
of headlights in the sky. On the instant, he had another
mental picture: of little Ivy Manson, gagged, bound,
violated, strangled. What the hell was he thinking about, it
couldn't be *worse*?

He pulled into the side of the road as a policeman came
up.

"I'm sorry sir, but —"

"I'm Commander Gideon, they're expecting me," Gideon
said, and the policeman moved back hurriedly. "My wife
will stay here, she can move the car if it's in the way." He
got out, bent down and tried to smile reassuringly at Kate.
"We'll sort it out," he said, and straightened up. The policeman seemed awkward, a short, pale-faced man who looked
almost as if he should still be at school.

"Sorry I nearly moved you on, sir."

"Don't be," Gideon said. "Lesson one – never be sorry

about doing your job, but do it with as little fuss as you can. A grin will persuade a driver to move on quicker than a scowl or a threat. How're things here?"

"I don't think it looks too good, sir."

"Soon see," said Gideon. He strode to the corner, where a crowd of other people had gathered, neighbours, ambulance men, firemen. A fire-tender was in the middle of the street itself, another was at one side of the warehouse and hoses were being run out, but there was no sign of fire. Gideon saw the warehouse gates wide open. Men saw and recognised him, no one attempted to stop him as he strode on, massive as a bear. He saw Carson, talking to an enormously fat woman, and then he came within sight of the main scene.

A big truck was drawn up in a corner by the loading bays. It was in such a position that no one could get at it, except from the front; it had almost certainly been parked there for the night. Police cars and motor cycles surrounded the bonnet and lights shone glaringly on to the windscreen, the cabin, and the man sitting at the wheel. At first, Gideon was interested only in what would happen if the man did what he threatened. He could send that truck leaping forward, scattering everyone in his path, and it was a ten-tonner; a lot of people would get hurt. He could swing out of the warehouse gateway – there were no gates – and into the street, where police cars were already drawn up. He wouldn't get far, but if he did reach the street there was no telling what damage he might do.

Then Gideon saw the man clearly, and recognised the beetle-browed driver he had seen that afternoon, the man he had thought looked the Lombroso type. And he had actually reproved himself for thinking so!

Carson said: "Good evening, Commander. I regret that it was necessary to call you out."

"Nothing you could do about it," Gideon said, and looked at the revoltingly fat woman. He doubted whether he had ever seen anyone with wider hips or a vaster body; she was obscenely fat, so enormous that it was difficult to imagine her as a woman with a normal figure, more like a grotesque balloon blown up to the point of bursting. Her hair was straggly, she was as ugly as proverbial sin, her little eyes glittered in the bright lights. She looked like a fat old witch.

"This is Miss Briggs, the man's sister," Carson introduced.

"Evening, Miss Briggs," Gideon said. "Think your brother will do what he threatens?"

"He's mad enough to do anything," the fat woman declared. "He'll do it all right." She had an unexpectedly pleasant voice, a little deeper than most women's. "Take it from me, I never gave it a thought until tonight, but now I can understand it. Used to scare my friends off, Jack did, even when he was a kid. Used to try to get *me* to have fun and games with him, too. He —"

"I have a public address outfit laid on," Carson interrupted her, "and I have warned Briggs twice of what will happen if he refuses to give himself up."

When he stopped, the humming of the truck's engine sounded very loud. There was little other noise, only an occasional footstep, an occasional cough. It was an absurd situation in some ways, with at least a hundred men already gathered near the van, and Briggs at the wheel holding them at bay because he could so easily kill two or three of them.

"Do you live with him?" Gideon asked.

"Ma and Pa live with *us*, if that's what you mean."

"Where are they?"

"Away for the week, thank God," said the woman. "God knows what they'll feel like when they know about this."

"Will your brother listen to them?" asked Gideon.

"They're down in Cornwall, he'd have a job to."

"Anyone else he'll listen to?"

"No, I can't say —" began Briggs's sister, and then something caught her eye, and she stared past Gideon, her ugly mouth dropping open and showing several discoloured teeth and one or two bare gums. Carson moved his head sharply, and Gideon saw that he was almost as shaken as the woman. Gideon turned round, deliberately unhurried. He saw a little elderly woman with grey hair coming across the cobbles of the yard. Two policemen were immediately behind her, and a tall woman, rather like Kate in height and figure, was with the policemen.

"For God's sake, get *her* away," Briggs's sister said hoarsely.

"It's Ivy Manson's mother," Carson told Gideon. He moved forward, to get in the woman's path. Mrs. Manson did not seem to notice him; she was staring fixedly at the man at the wheel of the truck. Yet she must have seen Carson, for she moved to one side, as if to try to evade him. The two policemen and the fat woman were very close behind her. Carson put out a hand and took her arm.

"I'm sorry, Mrs. Manson," he said, stiffly, "but you're not allowed in here. Go back with Mrs. Carter, please."

"That man killed my daughter," Mrs. Manson announced.

"We can't be sure of that, Mrs. Manson, and —"

"That man killed my daughter," she interrupted. Her voice was pitched on a high key, and there was no fluctuation in its tone. "He did terrible things to her, and then he killed her. I'm going to —"

"Mrs. Manson," said Carson firmly, "I'm sorry, but you can't come any further. Mrs. Carter, will you please —"

The elderly woman with the staring eyes snatched at the V of her blouse, and to Gideon's astonishment, to the horror of everyone close enough to see what was happening, she whipped out a carving knife. In the white glare of the headlights it looked vicious, cruel and deadly. She slashed at Carson's hand, and he hadn't a chance to escape the blade. Gideon shouted, but was just too far away to help. Carson drew in a hissing breath. Mrs. Manson broke away, and darted towards the truck. Gideon was nearest to her, and could have stopped her, but he let her go on. She ran over the cobbles as if they were as smooth as a race track, brandishing the knife in front of her. Gideon saw the glitter in Briggs's eyes, saw his mouth open, knew that Mrs. Manson had done what the crowd of men could not. He waited until Mrs. Manson reached the door of the cabin and clutched at the handle, then raced towards the other side. Briggs was glaring at the woman and the knife, and did not realise the second threat until Gideon wrenched open the door. Gideon hadn't much room, but he drove his fist into Briggs's stomach, and brought the man gasping forward over the wheel. Several policemen reached the other side, dragging Mrs. Manson away. Gideon put a foot against the floor of the cabin of the truck, leaned inside, took Briggs's left wrist, and twisted so that the man could not move. Then other policemen scrambled in on the far side, and Gideon let the wrist go, heard the click of handcuffs, and turned away.

Mrs. Manson was in the middle of a little group of people, including two policemen, the tall woman, and Kate. Kate. The bereaved woman was struggling and screaming and kicking out, Gideon thought she was actually foaming at the mouth. Carson was standing with two men, one of them pressing a thumb on the artery just above the crook in the elbow. There was a lot of blood on the back of his hand, and he looked much more pale than usual. Gideon expected him to faint.

Then a big plainclothes man from the Division got behind Mrs. Manson and pinioned her arms. Her screams were high-pitched and ear-splitting; maniacal. Her face was working, in the struggle her dress had been ripped off at one shoulder and on one side she was naked down to the stiff, steel supported corsets which held her bosom up.

"Where the hell's a doctor?" Gideon was muttering. "Where the hell —" he broke off, seeing men come hurrying, among them the Dr. Forbeson who had drawn up in a Rover that morning. It wasn't long before a needle thrust into the raving woman's arm brought almost instantaneous quiet, and not long before Carson was being attended by a doctor and two ambulance men. Gideon heard a doctor say:

"It'll need a stitch or two, we'll get him to hospital."

Carson moistened his lips.

"I am sorry about this, Commander," he said in a low pitched voice, "but my deputy is fully briefed and capable of carrying on. I hope that no one will blame the woman. Certainly I would not consider a charge is called for."

"She won't be charged," Gideon said.

He wondered if Mrs. Manson would ever be sane again, for he had never seen a clearer case of a woman driven out of her mind by shock and horror.

It was a little before eight o'clock when the last of the clearing up was done, most of the police had gone, both of the ambulances, the fire-tenders, the reporters. When Gideon reached his car, the policeman he had spoken to earlier was standing by it, and he opened Kate's door quickly. Gideon said: "Good night," and the constable gave him a broad smile and a hearty: "Good night, sir, and thank you!" Gideon drove off, slowly at first, and neither he nor Kate spoke. He was in Tottenham Court Road when he flicked on his radio, called Information Room, and asked:

"I want all the information I can get about Mrs. Manson, Mr. Carson, and Briggs. I'll be waiting for it with my radio on."

"Very good, sir," a man said, and Gideon left the radio crackling slightly, rather like a car receiver which was suffering badly from static.

"George," Kate said, quietly, "don't ever let me try to stop you from doing what you have to do."

Gideon said: "I'm not worried about that, Kate."

"I tried tonight," Kate said. "I almost hated the Yard." They went on for several minutes, along Oxford Street where most of the lights were green, where there was little traffic, and where only a few hundred people strolled past the brightly lit windows of a few shops, and the uninviting darkness of many others. "What would have happened if you hadn't gone? If you hadn't been able to?"

"Can't imagine anything that would have stopped me, even if I'd hated going," Gideon said, and went on thoughtfully: "If I hadn't been there, Carson or one of the others would have worked it out. I don't fool myself thinking that I'm really needed on a job like that. It's not just a question of being there to do anything, it's a question of, well, responsibility, I suppose. Someone would have had to give the order to close in on Briggs, and I'm the obvious man. If I'd been at home, well —"

"Who would have blamed you?"

"I would," answered Gideon. He found it difficult to explain, even to Kate, and was a little surprised that she was forcing the question, until he glanced at her. The glow in her eyes told him that she wasn't simply asking questions, she was making him talk, to ease his mind. "That's enough of that," he growled. "If one of the girls is ill, where do you want to be? On the other side of London?"

"This is your London, isn't it?" Kate said, very quietly. "I don't think even you realise how you think, George. You just follow your conscience."

"If you're trying to get me into a soft mood over that young fool of a son of ours —"

"Believe it or not I wasn't thinking about Matthew," said Kate. "I wouldn't have believed it possible, but I actually forgot him for half an hour tonight."

"*Calling Mr. Gideon*," a voice announced over the radio. "*Calling Mr. Gideon*."

"Gideon speaking," Gideon said quickly.

"Information Room reporting, sir, on the KL job, as requested. The prisoner, John Stewart Briggs, has made a full statement admitting his guilt, and is now being examined by Dr. Emmanuel." Emmanuel was the Yard's own psychiatrist, today as essential as a pathologist in criminal investigation. "Superintendent Carson has had eleven stitches in his right arm and the back of his hand, and will be at the North London Hospital for several days. He —"

Gideon interrupted: "Anyone told his wife?"

"Mr. Haydon here asked whether you wanted us to send someone, sir, or whether you —"

"I'll tell her," Gideon said, briskly, and glanced at Kate as he pulled into the left of the road and slowed down. "Check that he lives at 180, Marylebone Road." He let a stream of traffic past, and then swung round in a U turn.

"We'll be back in time for Matthew," he assured Kate. "Don't worry."

Driving on, he wondered whether he was really trying to delay talking and thinking about Matthew; whether he wasn't taking refuge in his job.

CHAPTER X

TED MIALL

THE moment that Carson's wife opened the door of the flat in St. John's Wood, one of a small block of post-war apartments, she sensed that this meant bad news. She knew Gideon only slightly, chiefly through meeting him at social functions arranged by the Yard. Kate, just behind him, remembered vividly that when she had first been introduced to the woman, she had been astonished that a cold-blooded, aloof man like Carson should have married a warm-blooded woman of Italian extraction, with quite beautiful dark eyes and a lovely, slightly olive complexion. She had lovely hair, too; dark, glossy, feathery.

"It's all right, Mrs. Carson," Gideon said, and his smile as well as the tone of his voice held reassurance. "I was out this way and thought I'd come and tell you what's happened, but it's nothing really serious."

"Is Sydney hurt?"

"Yes, but not —"

"You must come in, please," Mrs. Carson interrupted, and led them into a living-room which was beautifully appointed, with a colour scheme of pale green and grey, a thick pile carpet almost as white as snow, a grand piano taking up one corner and with a pale, polished sycamore case. "How badly is he hurt, Mr. Gideon?"

"He's got a nasty cut in his arm and he's had some

stitches. He's in hospital now, but it's only a matter of a few days."

"I understand," Mrs. Carson said. She sat down rather heavily on the edge of a silver grey brocaded settee, and brushed a hand across her forehead; the more Kate studied her, the more attractive she seemed. "It is very good of you to come and tell me yourself, Mr. Gideon. Like Sydney I expect you are very busy. He works too hard, I think." After a pause, she went on, "When Sydney left, he told me that he expected you would come to Islington. Please tell me, is that man caught?"

"Yes," Gideon answered. "It wasn't the man who did this, it was your husband trying to help . . ."

He explained, with an economy of words which report-making and reading had taught him, and he probably did not realise how vivid he made the picture. By the time he had finished, Mrs. Carson had recovered from the first shock. She got up to get some drinks, and then quite suddenly swirled round, hands raised in a kind of alarm, and exclaimed:

"But you have not had dinner?"

"We've had a snack," Gideon said hastily. "We don't —"

"Oh, please, you must stay. I was waiting for Sydney — he is often very late home for dinner. I was not hungry, I hoped he would perhaps be home in time, but he will not be, and the dinner will be wasted. It will not take long."

"You're very good," Gideon said, "but —"

"We'd love to stay," Kate decided for him, "but we have to be back at ten o'clock, one of our children will be waiting for us."

"But that is easy, it will be early enough if you leave here at half past nine, that is plenty of time," declared Mrs. Carson. "If you will just excuse me for a few minutes, everything is ready. Lia, my maid, she will be very glad." She hurried out, as if she were delighted. Gideon put his head on one side and said to Kate:

"Don't blame me."

"It will help her to get over the shock," Kate said. "If I

were in her shoes, I'd much rather be too busy for an hour than sitting and thinking about you."

"Have it your own way," Gideon said. "I've got a feeling that it's going to be quite a meal, too. Carson really does himself proud, doesn't he?"

"Envious?" Kate asked.

"I can't imagine anything I would like less than to have no children," Gideon said, and added gruffly: "Even to-night."

It was five minutes to ten when Gideon swung the car into his own street and drew up outside his house. A light in the hall and one at a small bedroom window – Priscilla's window – did not tell them whether Matthew was in. There was no light on at the front of the Mialls' house, a few doors along. Gideon reached Kate's door as she started to climb out, said: "Now I'm for it," and led the way to the front door, taking out his keys. He wasn't looking forward to this interview at all. Kate would make sure that he was not interrupted, but it was a pity he would have to use the front room, because that would make the other children wonder what was up. A discreet word about 'Cambridge' might satisfy them. He heard footsteps along the street, of a man and a woman, and as he opened the door, Kate whispered:

"*George.*"

He turned his head. "What?"

"They're both coming."

"*What?*" Gideon stared along the street and saw Matthew passing beneath a street lamp, with Helen by his side. They were walking a few inches apart from each other, as if making sure that their arms and legs did not touch. "Damn it, she'll go home, won't she?" said Gideon, as Kate said hastily:

"Don't stand staring at them. Get indoors."

Inside the passage, Gideon said lugubriously: "Did he say he was going to bring her?"

"He didn't say one thing or the other."

"*Mother!*" Priscilla called, from her bedroom. "Is that you? I'll be down in a minute."

"All right, 'Silla," Kate called, and added to Gideon: "I
bet Malcolm is doing his homework and looking at the
television at the same time, that boy will never get on if we
can't make him concentrate. You let them in, I'll make sure
that the coast is clear."

"Kate, don't you think you —"

"I'll come in after a quarter of an hour," said Kate, as
the footsteps stopped outside, and then sounded again on
the path leading to the front door.

Kate went along to the kitchen, while Matthew, who had
a key, stood hesitating on the front doorstep. There was a
whisper of voices before the key sounded in the lock. Gideon
put on the light of the front room, with its shiny mahogany
furniture, its deep settee and rather formal comfort, and
went in. He thrust his right hand into his pocket and
smoothed the bowl of his pipe much as he would at the
office when he was expecting a difficult interview. Then
Matthew came in, and said in a muted voice:

"I'll just see where they are."

"All right," whispered Helen.

"I'm in here, Matthew," Gideon said, and failed completely to keep the harsh note out of his voice. It was going
to be very difficult to keep a balance in this situation, and
he reminded himself that he had to be objective and
rational, and that nothing must be done in haste. "Come in,
the pair of you," he went on.

Matthew came in first, looked at his father very straightly,
and then stood aside for Helen. She also stared straight at
Gideon, but went pink as she did so; Matthew had two red
spots against the pallor of his cheeks. Matthew looked much
more spick and span than usual, Helen was made up as for
an occasion, wearing a very pale lipstick, just then in vogue.
As Matthew closed the door, she moved towards Gideon,
only a little hesitantly. She had certainly matured. The
loose coat which draped from her shoulders and fell open at
the front showed her small waist, rounded hips, and that
beautifully shaped, provocative little bosom. She was a
pretty thing, too, in a rather unusual way, with a heart-
shaped face, a slightly snub nose, and rounded blue eyes.

"Hallo, Helen," Gideon said.

"Mr. Gideon, I hope you won't mind if I say something first," said Helen. "I've been thinking of it ever since Matt and I decided that we ought both to come and face you together."

"Carry on," conceded Gideon.

"Thank you," Helen said, with gravity far beyond her years. She had lost the flush, and was even more pale than Matthew. Her skin was very clear and without blemish, rather as if it were transparent. "It's just this, Mr. Gideon. It was just as much my fault as Matthew's, and I *am* a year older."

"Hmm," grunted Gideon. "I daresay you're right – sit down, do – and even I know that it takes two to create a situation like this." He looked across at Matthew, who was standing stiffly, not quite at attention. Helen sat down.

"How old are you, Helen?"

That gained a moment or two.

"Nearly twenty," Helen answered. "And I have thought about this, Mr. Gideon. I am old enough to know what it all implies."

"Yes," said Gideon. "Yes, obviously you are." He glanced at his son. "Are you, Matthew?"

"I think so, sir." Matthew hadn't called him 'sir' for years.

"I gather that you've some idea that in spite of this, you don't feel obliged to get married," Gideon said. "Aren't you overdoing the cynical attitude?"

"I don't think so," answered Helen quickly; whether Matthew liked it or not, he was going to have this interview managed for him. "The point is, Mr. Gideon, that everyone knows these days that there couldn't be a worse start for a marriage than to be under an obligation, or to be burdened with a baby almost from the beginning. It isn't what people would say and think, it isn't even what my – my parents would think." She faltered for the first time. "It's that it would probably ruin our lives. And at the moment, I can't think of anyone I would like to marry less than Matthew. I think he feels the same about me."

"We – we feel we've got to chalk it up against experience," Matthew blurted out.

Gideon said heavily: "Oh, you do, do you?" He looked straight at his son, and he would never know that he looked exactly as he often did with a man in front of him at his office – one already charged or about to be charged with some serious offence. His voice grew deeper, rougher. "It's as simple as that, is it? Chalk it up to experience. Let me tell you, young man, that you've let Helen down, you've betrayed the trust of her parents, you've let your mother down with a hell of a bang, and you've made me feel thoroughly ashamed of my own flesh and blood. I didn't ever think that would happen." He saw Helen open her mouth, and waved her to silence. Matthew was standing absolutely still, eyes burning, the two spots vivid on his cheeks. "Don't you let me hear any more glib talk about chalking it up to experience. Apart from getting Helen into a lot of trouble and creating problems that might affect her for the rest of her life, you've behaved like a skunk. What do you think you've got reproductive glands for? To behave like a farmyard animal? You can help to create children, you can make a girl or a woman conceive, but man, woman and sex carry a hell of a lot more responsibility than you seem to think. A *man's* responsibility, and in some ways the biggest responsibility any man can carry. And no one else can help carry it for you. You'll make or mar your own life and you'll make and mar Helen's. I'm not going to rub it in any more than I have to, but if I hear any more talk or see any indication that you take it lightly or 'chalk it up to experience' I'll give you the hiding of your life." Gideon wiped his forehead, because he was suddenly warm; but he felt much better than when the interview had started. "Now come and sit down and start thinking about this like an adult, not a boy. As for you, Helen, you're going to hear all about it from your parents before long, and there's just one thing I want from you."

Matthew didn't move, but his eyes were shinier than ever, and he was clenching and unclenching his hands.

"What – what is that, Mr. Gideon?" Helen made herself ask.

"I want to know how I can help," Gideon said. "I'm more sorry than I can say that it's happened, but it has happened and it's partly my fault for not keeping a stricter eye on Matthew. Now, what can I do?"

He was startled when the door opened and Kate came in; startled because quite suddenly Helen's face began to pucker up, and she began to cry. Kate went straight across to her. Matthew was biting his lips. The music from the television seemed to be from another world.

"If – if – if only you'd break the news to my mother and father," Helen said, a few minutes later. "I just can't tell them myself, I'd rather die."

"Why, hallo, George," said Ted Miall, standing with his back to the hall of the house which was identical with Gideon's, except that it was in need of decorating and there were no signs of the improvements such as Gideon had carried out. "Come in, do. You're just in time for a cup of tea. Jane's putting the kettle on." He closed the door on Gideon, and led the way along the hall towards the kitchen, then said suddenly: "Or would you rather have a word in the front room? I can easily —"

"Who is it, Ted?" called Mrs. Miall.

"It's George Gideon. George —"

"I don't know whether either of you has any idea what I've come about," said Gideon, as Mrs. Miall hurried along, "but I hope you're not going to throw me out." He looked at the pair, both in the early fifties, a little faded, a little care-worn, a little thin-faced, rather earnest and solemn and very sober people. "If someone were coming to me with the same story I'd like Kate to be present, and I hope you will agree, Jane." He wanted to get it over. "The truth is —"

"So it was Matthew," Jane Miall said, in a dead-sounding voice.

"What —" began her husband, squeakily.

"That's what you've come about, George, isn't it?" asked Mrs. Miall. "Matthew and our Helen. Ted, I told you that

I didn't like the signs with Helen. I didn't like the way she went off her food in the morning, and —"

"Good gracious," Miall said, and the trite exclamation irritated Gideon. *"Matthew."*

"You'd better come and sit down," Jane Miall said. "It's no use standing in the hall like this, and *I* want a cup of tea."

As they went towards the kitchen, Miall said in a stronger voice: "Are you telling me that your son has taken advantage of my daughter, and — and put her with child?"

"I wish it weren't so, Ted," Gideon said, "but it is."

"Why, it's outrageous! It —"

"Teddy, it wasn't *George,*" protested Jane Miall, and Gideon looked at her in fresh understanding and appreciation. They went into a bleak, bare living-room-cum-kitchen, where an open fire sent out a fierce, roasting heat.

"Sit down, George," Mrs. Miall said. "Who told you — or did you or Kate find out?"

Gideon began to talk.

Ted Miall said very little, and that little was almost comical; he certainly knew all the stock phrases. But Gideon felt a stirring of hope that his wife would show real understanding and realise that the youngsters had never needed help and guidance as they did now. A censorious attitude might easily drive them into doing something silly, perhaps dangerous. Gideon sipped tea, while Miall let his get cold in his cup. It was stiflingly hot, and the fire seemed to grow fiercer. When Gideon had finished, it was Miall who said:

"Well, there's only one possible solution. They must get married as soon as they can. There is no reason why they shouldn't have the banns called and be married within three weeks, there are plenty of premature babies. There's no need for a special licence. My goodness, if they'd waited much longer before telling us, everyone would have known! We've lived here eighteen years, and in all that time nothing like this has ever happened to one of *my* family."

"Ted," Gideon said, very heavily, "they don't want to get married."

"They don't *what*?"

"George, I think it would be better if you were to go and fetch Helen," said Jane Miall. "Then when we've had a talk with her, we can discuss it again in the morning. Tell Helen she needn't worry, though."

"You can tell Helen and you can tell your son that they haven't any choice," declared Miall, angrily. "They've got to get married at the earliest possible moment. Your son's got to do the right thing by my daughter, and the sooner he makes up his mind to it the better." He glared into Gideon's eyes, a smaller, frailer man, the kind of man Gideon could make two of, but there was a strength in him which Gideon saw and understood; a stubbornness which he had known and feared. "And I shall expect you to bring all the necessary pressure to bear on your son," Miall went on. "He's betrayed our trust, that's what he's done. If I had my way, I would give him a thorough thrashing."

"I know how you feel," Gideon said.

"George, will you bring Helen home?" asked Jane Miall.

Gideon went out of the house slowly, leaving the door ajar, hearing Miall talking the moment he thought that it was safe from being overheard. "I don't care what you say, they'll have to do right by our child...."

Kate was at the gate.

Gideon gave her the drift of what had passed between him and the Mialls, and she nodded thoughtfully, and said:

"It's about what we'd expect. Leave Helen to me now, George."

He was only too glad to obey, and followed her into the house and the front room, where Helen and Matthew were sitting stiffly on either side of the fireplace with its big over-mantel mirror. Helen jumped up.

"How did they take it?" she burst out.

"Helen, I think you've got to make up your mind to a trying few days," Kate said. "Your father is very upset, and your mother deeply hurt, of course. You'll have to be extremely patient, especially with your father. When he's talking, no matter how much you disagree with what he says, you've got to remember that it is you and Matthew, not your mother and father, who are responsible for the situation. You will have to be very, very humble."

"I – I know," Helen said huskily. "I will be."

"I'll come back with you," Kate offered, and a few minutes later, Matthew was left alone with his father. By now it was obvious that Priscilla and Malcolm were aware that something exceptional was up, and Gideon wondered whether it would be wiser to tell the whole family; at least it would stop whispering and prying. He must talk to Kate about that.

"Well, son," he said gruffly.

"I – I didn't mean that ch-ch-chalk it up the way it sounded," Matthew muttered. "I do realise what a heel I've been, Dad. I do really. Do you think Mr. Miall will insist on us getting married right away?"

"I think we'll all have to spend a few days thinking it out and trying to make sure what's best," Gideon said. "You'll have to wear sackcloth and ashes for a while, anyhow. Tell me this: is Helen the first girl you've known in this way?"

"Good lord, yes!"

"Did anything lead up to it, apart from having too much to drink on New Year's Eve?"

"You mean, did anything happen between Helen and me before that? Well, no," answered Matthew, and he flushed. "As a matter of fact, Dad, I first thought of Helen as a – as a woman, if you see what I mean, when we were out in a party at Maidenhead in September. You remember, there was a very hot week-end, and a dozen of us went. I'd never really noticed Helen before, not – not her body, I mean. I'd noticed plenty of other women and like most chaps made a few jokes about vital statistics, but Helen was wearing a bikini. Everyone made a joke about it, but she was a bit embarrassed, and told me afterwards that she hadn't realised it was so small. She'd bought it last year, and – well, she'd got bigger. Somehow from then on I was interested in her. We went to the pictures now and again, and the tennis club dances. But there wasn't anything serious, until New Year's Eve. Well, New Year's Day really."

"All right, son," Gideon said gruffly. "I'll do all I can to help work this thing out the best way." He admitted that he was stalling even himself, but that was what he most wanted; to be able to consider the situation when it was possible to feel calm, when the shock effect had gone.

As he spoke, the telephone bell rang. He glanced at his watch, saw that it was nearly half past eleven, and hoped that this wasn't a call that would take him out. The last thing he wanted was to leave Kate on her own tonight.

It was KL Division.

"Information at the Yard asked me to call you, sir," the man said. "They said you'd left instructions to be informed about Mrs. Manson."

"Yes?"

"A Dr. Forbeson has just reported to the Division, sir, and says that he doesn't think there is very much one can do for Mrs. Manson for the time being. She's still very violent. Quite off her rocker, sir, if you know what I mean."

"I know what you mean," Gideon said heavily. "All right, thanks. What about Manson?"

"He's taking it on the chin," the man answered. "Apparently he's staying with some neighbours. You knew that Briggs made a full confession, didn't you?"

"Yes," said Gideon. "All right, thanks." He rang off, and immediately dialled the Yard, aware that Matthew was alone in the front room, and in the kitchen Priscilla and Malcolm were whispering.

"What kind of a night is it?" Gideon inquired of the Information Officer who answered:

"Pretty quiet," said Information. "Five drunks in Piccadilly started a fight but they're all cooling their heels, now. There was a fire over at Canning Town, but it was put out before it spread much. A jeweller's window in —"

"All right, thanks," said Gideon, for he heard Kate coming in. He watched her closing the door, and thought of the screaming woman at the warehouse, and the probability that she had been driven insane. He thought of the fire which had been put out, and found himself thinking again of the eight victims of the fire at Lambeth. Eight, remember, and tonight he had hardly given them a thought. There was one consolation: he could be sure that Lucky Margetson had.

Kate beckoned, Gideon went with her into the front room, where Matthew was sitting on an upright chair, his eyes still feverishly bright. Kate closed the door briskly, and said:

"Mrs. Miall will help Helen all she can, and we'll all feel better when we've slept on it. I told Priscilla that there was some talk of the two of you wanting to get married, and that will satisfy her and everyone else. It would be quite enough to cause a family upheaval. Don't snap at them if they ask questions, Matthew, just try to laugh it off. Don't you agree, George?"

"Absolutely," Gideon said. He had never appreciated his wife so much.

Tony Harrison was thinking about his wife, too, at that very moment, and he was talking to himself.

"I could make her take them myself," he said. "I could stand over her while she took them, force them down her neck if necessary. My God, that's it! I'll wait until she starts moaning about not sleeping, and —"

His thoughts broke suddenly, and he stood very still. Then he said in a soft voice:

"No I won't. I'll mix a dozen sleeping tablets in some hot rum, she won't know there's anything wrong with the flavour. The very first chance I get."

He put his right hand to his pocket, and touched a box of sleeping tablets which the doctor had prescribed for his wife a few months ago, just after Tim had left for the army. Two at night at the very most, the doctor had warned.

Everyone knew how unhappy Pamela had been because the kids had left home. No one would really be surprised that she killed herself.

CHAPTER XI

WEEK OF ANXIETY

WHEN Gideon reached his office next morning, Saturday, Joe Bell was there with a pile of reports in front of him, and a bigger pile already stood on Gideon's desk. They said, "'Morning, Joe, 'Morning George," and Gideon took off his coat and draped it over a chair, then mechanically pulled his tie loose. He stared at the pile of reports as he sat in front of the desk, and said:

"What's happened? Every jail opened to let 'em all get busy at once?"

"It's the last Saturday in April, George."

"Oh, Gawd, so it is," said Gideon, and was annoyed with himself because he had not prepared himself for this on the way from Hurlingham. Usually he would have, but this morning he had been too preoccupied with Matthew and Helen, partly because he had bumped into Miall on the way to the garage. Miall had started the 'I-don't-care-what-anyone-says-George' gambit and Gideon had lost ten minutes and nearly lost his temper. The worst of it was that he could fully understand the distress in the other man's mind.

The last Saturday in every month had developed into a kind of spring cleaning day. Every pending case on the Yard's file was looked at, as was every case coming up for remand at the Magistrate's Court and every case being prepared for the criminal courts. Gideon made a practice of taking a bagful of files home, to look at during the week-end, so that he could decide what tactics to use, and start using them on Monday. There simply wasn't time to do everything he had to do during the week.

"Anything new?" he asked.

"Nothing that matters. You heard about Mrs. Manson?"

"Yes."

"Nasty business," Bell said. "Briggs will be up at North London this morning, just a formal charge and hearing. I'm leaving that to the Division."

"Good."

"Margetson telephoned. He still hasn't traced that second cyclist. The fires were in places owned by different people – one by the Ecclesiastical Commissioners, two by the London County Council, two privately. He sounded a bit dispirited."

"Lucky won't, for long."

"Riddell phoned from Chichester. He says that Harrison seems to be having a serious affaire with this Chloe Duval. There's a chance that the second body in that quarry grave can be identified through an old toe fracture, the Brighton pathologist says that she must have had hammer toes when she was young, and had an operation to break them and straighten them. If it was a Brighton job, he can find out. If not there are about a thousand operations of the same kind every year, at a rough guess."

"Let's hope it's a Brighton job."

"Riddell's working at it. He's staying down over the week-end."

Gideon grunted. "Probably means he's going to have his wife down there. Has he forgotten that this Chloe Duval might be Harrison's next victim?"

"He says they're having too good a time for anything to happen yet. If he takes her out to that quarry or anywhere quiet – but you said that yourself."

"I know, that's the big danger," conceded Gideon. He paused, and then asked: "Any word about Jarvis's funeral?"

"Monday, two o'clock," answered Bell, and went on: "It's going to be at Eltham Cemetery, and the Millers will be in the next plots – all of them. Mrs. Jarvis has agreed. I think she feels it will be a kind of permanent tribute."

"Make sure I leave here by one o'clock," said Gideon gruffly, "I'll find out if the A.C. intends to come, too. Anything much in during the night?"

"Only routine stuff."

"We could do with a week of routine," Gideon remarked, almost wistfully, and glanced through the top files, all of new cases. There was only a limited briefing session on Saturday mornings, all but urgent work being set aside for the week-end clean up. Briefing done, he settled down to a study of the pending cases, finding very few of immediate interest. Then he came to the old-standing one of the murder of the night watchman at Bournemouth. He read this closely, then studied Cornish's files on the bank tunnelling job and the murder of Beatrice Clapper. He looked up.

"What about the response to the television appeal?"

"Fair. Cornish is interviewing all the likely people over at NE," answered Bell. "He's going to call us about eleven."

"Anything in from that solicitor, Lewisham?"

"Meant to tell you, he's over at Brixton now, with Clapper. Nice client to have."

Gideon grunted again, and turned back to the files. Occasionally he took out his pipe and stuck it in the corner of his mouth, but he did not fill it. Bell was sifting patiently through cases which would be referred to him before the morning was over. As often happened on Saturday, the telephones were fairly quiet – the Yard worked, but the closing of most offices in the City and West End meant that they had a quieter time. It was half past ten, and Gideon was nearly through, when there was a bang on the door, and it swung open, almost at the same instant. Lemaitre strode in, bright-eyed, perky, wearing a red and blue spotted bow tie. Lemaitre's suit was a little too bright a blue, his shoes too gingery a brown, and as always he had something of the look of an eager boy.

"George, what do you think's turned up *now*?"

"What?" asked Gideon. "Ericson jumped off Waterloo Bridge?"

"When I worked here, I used to keep him up to his job," Lemaitre complained to Bell. "He didn't have time to be bloody flippant. Roscoe's back in circulation. How about *that*? He spent the night before last at the Ericson's place, now Ericson and he've gone to their office this morning. There's another queer thing, too."

"What's queer about people working?"

"The office staff's not in this morning," Lemaitre retorted. "The two bosses are there alone. The other queer thing affects Mrs. Ericson, who's quite a doll," Lemaitre went on. "One of the long shanked, lean hipped, quiet —"

"Thinking of dating her, so as to get the low-down on her husband?"

"Now put a cork in it, Gee-Gee," Lemaitre protested, rising to the bait. "She's done a tour of relatives and friends, that's what she's done."

"What kind of a tour?" demanded Gideon.

"Had a chap following her yesterday, and I've just seen his report," said Lemaitre. "She made seven calls yesterday, all of them on relations, and some of the relations are pretty well-heeled. Something's up."

"What've you done?"

"I haven't done anything else yet, can't be sure I'll get the moral support of my superiors," Lemaitre said caustically. "But I can tell you what I think, George."

"Go on."

"What I *think*," said Lemaitre, striding closer to the desk, placing both hands on it, and thrusting his bony face towards Gideon's, "is that they're raising all the dough they can. It's a big borrowing spree, blood-thicker-than-water kind of thing. And I think that within a day or two, possibly today or tomorrow, they'll all get out of the country. They're getting ready to run, George."

"I wonder," said Gideon thoughtfully.

"Goddammit, it speaks for itself!"

"Does it?" asked Gideon. He did not remark that there was only one reason why Lemaitre had been so late getting promotion to superintendency, and now had no hope of reaching the top. Lemaitre was shrewd, clever, patient, and painstaking but just a little too reckless; nothing cured him of jumping to conclusions. On at least three occasions he had been up before the Assistant Commissioner for making an arrest on insufficient evidence, and so he had learned the lesson of listening to advice; but he chafed under it.

"Listen, George, be reasonable," he pleaded. "The Ericsons are broke and so is the firm. Roscoe's been away, obviously spying out the land. They're in the red for fifty thousand quid, and once we establish that the surveyor reports were faked and the issue a fraud, we've got 'em cold. They know it, all right, but they probably know it will be some time before we can get all the evidence we want, too. At the moment we can't stop them from going abroad, unless we charge them."

"Got proof about the surveyor's reports being faked?"

"It's only a matter of time, George!"

"I daresay," said Gideon.

"If we lose that precious trio —"

"Last time I read your report you said that there was no indication that Mrs. Ericson was involved," Gideon told him. "Now she's a chief plotter. What do you want to do?"

"Go and see Roscoe this morning, and let him have it straight from the shoulder."

After a pause, Gideon said: "No. No, Lem, not yet. I daresay you're right on the overall picture, but if you see Roscoe now and don't get any kind of admission from him, there's a risk that you'll warn him off. I'll tell you what. Detail four men to the job, and watch all three of the suspects. If they buy air or sea tickets, or if they turn up at one of the airports or the channel ports – any port for that matter – have 'em held for questioning. If they don't try to get away, we may have to do some more thinking."

"Well, at least you admit they might try to do a flit," grumbled Lemaitre, and then rubbed his hands. "We'll have all three of 'em by Monday, they'll try to go all right. Thanks, George. See you picked up that Islington swine, Briggs."

"Yes."

"How's Carson?"

"Good God!" exclaimed Gideon. "I forgot to check!" He sent an almost horrified glance at Bell, who smiled his rather fatherly smile and said:

"He had a comfortable night, and if his wife tries hard enough she can get him home today. The official advice is

that he should stay in the hospital over the week-end, more
to rest than anything else. That's one of the things I've been
meaning to talk about, George."

"That's right, let Uncle Joe look after you," gibed
Lemaitre. "Talk about reminding me about old times."

"What is, Joe?" asked Gideon.

"There hasn't been much trouble out at KL," said Bell,
quietly. "It's ticked over very smoothly. There was that
policeman killing last year, when Carson did a damned
good job, and since then it's run itself." Gideon realised
that Bell was right on the ball; he himself had not been to
KL very often, not only because there was little official
need, but also because he had not liked Carson very much.
"I had the Deputy Divisional Superintendent on the blower
for a long time last night," Bell went on. "He didn't want
to worry you, or rather he wanted me to worry you!"
Bell's smile was even more fatherly, even benign. "He says
that Carson's been working himself to death. Won't leave
anything to juniors, if he can help it, spends far too much
time at the Division by night – over-conscientious, that's the
simple word. Whenever he's going off for a day or two, he
always leaves precise instructions, and he hasn't had a clear
week off for eighteen months. I checked, and that's right."

"Hmm," said Gideon, heavily.

"The D.D.S. says this might be a good chance to make
him take a month off," said Joe.

"Yes," agreed Gideon. "I'll fix it." He remembered how
Carson had said, almost desperately, that his deputy was
fully briefed. He remembered how Carson's lovely wife had
said that she was so used to waiting late for her husband,
and that her Sydney worked too hard. And he thought of
the austerity of the Divisional Superintendent, that aloof-
ness, that withdrawness. Here was a case where he himself
had been fooled by the smooth way in which the Division
ran; he should have been over at KL much more often,
getting to know Carson better. He would have, had there
been a lot of badly-handled cases. He made a mental note
to talk to Mrs. Carson, and said: "Thanks, Joe. What are

you waiting for, Lem? I thought you wanted to make sure
the Ericsons and Roscoe were watched."

"Pooh, I laid that on before I came in," said Lemaitre.
"Anything much in, George? All right if I go off a bit early
today? I've only five weeks' leave due, I don't really deserve
an hour off, but —"

"See you Monday, Lem."

"Ta," said Lemaitre, and breezed out.

"I believe we can do it," Roscoe was saying, about that
time. "If you're sure that your Uncle Reggie can be relied
on for ten thousand, I believe we can do it. Joan, I didn't
think you were right, you know damned well I didn't, but
by God, I've come to the conclusion that I'd rather clean
boots or dig ditches than stand trial. I wonder if we can put
it across to the police."

"If we can make quite sure of returning all the invest-
ments, they'll believe us," said Ericson, rather too loudly.

"I hope to God you're right," Roscoe said. "Anyway,
we've got to draft that letter to the customers. How we've
found that there was an error in the reports, that there isn't
as much iron, that in the circumstances . . ."

The next morning, Sunday, 'Mr. Brown' had his breakfast in bed. Mrs. Tennison had made a practice of taking
Sunday breakfast up to him, a little after nine o'clock, with
two newspapers, the *Sunday Globe* and the *Sunday Mail*.
She saw him sitting up and looking through a Bible, of which
she fully approved, and he gave her a pleasant smile as he
put this down, and hitched himself up in bed. She thought
he seemed much better. Earlier in the week, his eyes had
been red-rimmed and he had looked as if he was sickening
for something – she remembered how he had been affected
by the story of the fire which had killed the Millers. But he
was obviously over that now.

When he saw her close the door, he snatched the *Sunday
Globe* and looked through it quickly. There was a huge
display about the fire at Hilton Terrace, obviously inspired

by the police. There were photographs of all the victims, including Jarvis, and the headline screamed:

WHY DID FIREBUG MURDER THESE PEOPLE?

Then he saw a footnote; *see editorial*. He turned over the pages hurriedly, and saw the leading article was headed:

FIRE TRAPS

His eyes glistened as he read a violent attack on housing conditions in some parts of London, phrases like 'a living disgrace in a civilised community', and 'This must strike the conscience of every man who has a safe house of his own'.

"It's working," Mr. Brown gasped. "It's working at last, and – it is because they *died*."

He thrust the newspaper aside, and snatched up the *Sunday Mail*. Here the headline ran:

MYSTERIOUS OUTBREAK OF EAST END FIRES

IS SAME FIRE-RAISER RESPONSIBLE?

He moistened his lips, put this aside, then started on the bacon and eggs, which were already cold on his plate. When he had finished he said in a small, clear voice:

"If anyone murdered those people, the landlord did. I was only the instrument. The landlord murdered them, and now" – his eyes were shining with a kind of radiance – "and now someone is sitting up and taking notice. If people die, something will be done. At last they're *listening* to me." What he did not admit to himself was why something of the awful pain which had racked him since his wife and daughter had died, had eased since the Miller tragedy; it was as if some terrible pressure had been lifted from his mind. Hating the owners of the slums had not helped like this; planning to destroy more helped, though, and so did lying to himself. Telling himself that if he burned more

places and more people it would force the authorities to tear
down the fire-traps was the only way he could rationalise
what he was doing.

He knew one thing: he had to keep on, on, on; unless he
did he would know no peace within him.

He poured himself out a cup of lukewarm tea, then
picked up the *Globe* again. The front page story caught his
attention:

YARD CHIEF ACCUSED OF ASSAULTING PRISONER

'Brown' began to read.

At the Gideons' home, it was Matthew who collected the
newspapers that Sunday morning, a Matthew still very
subdued, and coltish in his anxiety to be as helpful as he
could in running errands and doing little household chores.
This morning, he had taken tea in to his parents, told them
he would see to their breakfast – Kate allowed the children
to get up whenever they wanted on Sunday morning, but
they had to get their own meal. All of them were up, all of
them had looked into the big bedroom, where Kate was
sitting up against the pillows of the double bed, and Gideon
was shrugging his arms into a dressing-gown.

"We can't put off another talk with the Mialls much
longer," Gideon said.

"I'm going to talk to Jane again this morning, she's making an excuse not to go to chapel," Kate said. "I don't like
the way Ted Miall's behaving, but there's another aspect
Jane did point out."

"What's that?"

"Why don't they want to get married?" Kate said, and
then raised a hand and went on hurriedly: "Listen, George!
Is it possible that they are simply reacting against a compulsion *to* get married? How fond would they be of each
other if it weren't for this baby?"

"If it weren't for this baby they wouldn't be giving a
thought to marriage," Gideon said, "and if they were, I'd
make sure they soon forgot it. The thing that troubles me

is the fact that they might marry, and be sorry all their lives. I'm not thinking simply of the scholarship, although that's a key point in some ways. If Matthew can't go up to Cambridge, the time might come when he'll blame Helen because he couldn't take advantage of the opportunity. Once that starts —"

"There's another possibility you've overlooked, George," Kate said. "They might marry and be thoroughly happy, and we'd be young grandparents. There's no real reason why being married should interfere with Cambridge —"

"Here! Am I to keep the *three* of them now?"

"We could help," Kate said quietly. "Helen would work for a few months, and work after the baby arrives if necessary. I've been thinking that Matt could do a lot worse for a wife, and we could do a lot worse for a daughter-in-law. What's more, the Mialls might help out a bit. They —"

"Hold it! I can hear Matt coming," Gideon interrupted.

A moment later, Matthew appeared in the doorway, carrying the Sunday newspapers. He looked startled and rather as he had when Gideon had first seen him about Helen. Two papers were tucked underneath his arm, the other was in his hands, for reading.

"Hallo, Matthew, what's startled you?" asked Kate.

Gideon thought: Miall hasn't been at him already this morning, has he?

Matthew said: "You're not going to like this, Dad, and I'd like to strangle the swine."

"Now, what —" began Kate, and Gideon got up and took the newspaper. There was the front page headline:

YARD CHIEF ACCUSED OF ASSAULTING PRISONER

"Well I'm —" began Gideon, explosively, and broke off.

"What *is* it?" demanded Kate.

"Some little runt of a solicitor says that Dad hit a man when he was questioning him about a bank hold-up," Matthew said, but Gideon hardly heard him or Kate as he read the story. It was quite simple and straightforward.

Clapper's solicitor had twisted the office incident exactly as
Gideon had realised was possible, and made a few elabora-
tions, each adding to the speciousness of the accusation.
There were photographs of Clapper, of his wife, and the
tie-in with the murder at Whitechapel. It was glaringly
obvious that the *Sunday Globe* had wanted a different
angle on the Whitechapel murder.

Gideon tossed the paper aside. Kate leaned forward and
picked it up.

"Didn't they check with you first?" she demanded.

"Might have called the back room inspector, but I doubt
it," Gideon said. "They'll say that they didn't get the story
until last night, and there was no one at the Yard who could
help them. Probably say they couldn't get any answer from
us. It's almost a pity," he added softly, "that it isn't true."

"That's an odd thing for you to say," Kate remarked.

Gideon said: "It is an odd case. Clapper's covering up
for the man who's letting him take the rap for the bank job,
and also for the man who killed his wife. See how low a
man can get, Matt?"

Matthew said: "What —" and then flushed a beetroot
red.

"No, George!" Kate protested.

"Eh?" Gideon looked up at his son, startled, and then
realised what they had inferred. "Oh, don't be a chump, I
wasn't getting at you, I was just being factual – or fatuous,"
he added. "I'd better get a bath and then have a hearty
breakfast, this is going to be quite a day."

"For a minute I thought you'd meant it for me," Matthew
said ruefully. "Dad, can't you sue this rag?"

"I could sue it if it made cracks about my private life, but
not for anything I do in the course of the job – unless I was
accused of corrupt practices. If a copper could sue for libel
or slander because of criticism of his job, we'd always be in
the Civil Courts. If you're serious about wanting to become
a policeman one of these days, you'll learn. Now, that
bath!"

The Assistant Commissioner telephoned while he was at
breakfast. Joe Bell, Lemaitre, and the Public Relations

Officer at the Yard also telephoned – all in the same strain, all angry, all trying to suggest the best thing to do. Daily newspapers began to call soon after ten o'clock. Two television news units asked for statements and interviews. A day which should have included a little gardening, repairs to the landing window, another talk with Matthew, and a refresher on the files of pending cases, was ruined. Gideon was allowed to think of practically nothing but the assault charge. To all newspapers and news units he gave a flat denial without explaining what had happened; the explanation would sound too much like that of a man with a black eye who said that a door had banged into him. He was surprised that Cornish didn't call, and by half past three that afternoon began to worry about him, for Cornish was usually very prompt. Two murders were already involved, and if a man would kill a woman to stop her from talking, what would he do to a policeman who came dangerously close? Gideon told himself that there was no need to worry, and yet he did worry.

At half past three there was another ring at the front door bell, and Matthew hurried to open it. Gideon had told him to tell any newspapermen that he was out, listened, and heard Cornish's voice. He got up. Matthew called out to say who it was, and led Cornish into the living-room. The Yard man was unshaven, his clothes were rumpled, and he looked bleary-eyed.

"Hallo, George," he said. "You've had a rough morning, I bet."

"What do you think you've had?"

"Oh, I just stayed up all night," said Cornish, "I've been checking every one of the people who thought they saw Beatrice Clapper. I kept that going until midnight, had a meal, and then drove down to Bournemouth. I thought there might be something in the local files on the night-watchman job that would help. Drew a blank, though. All I got for the day and the night's work was a vague description of the man who was seen with Mrs. C. near the docks about lunchtime on the day of the murder. Leaving out the lunatic fringe, the only report of a man seen leaving the

cul-de-sac at the time of the murder makes the killer a man
of the middle thirties, dressed like a docker or labourer. I
only picked up one thing which struck me as odd."

"What was it?"

"A boy leaving the yard saw a couple talking there and
said that he thought the man spoke to the woman in a 'posh'
voice."

Gideon didn't speak.

"If that's true, he was probably wearing a labourer's
clothes so as to look the part, and we need to look further
afield than the East End," Cornish went on. "I wondered if
that would be a good angle to tackle Clapper on."

"Seen Clapper?"

"Thought I'd better wait and find out what the official
reaction is to the *Sunday Globe*," Cornish said. "What are
you going to do, George?"

"Deny the story, and carry on normally," Gideon said.
"The A.C. agrees with me, our attitude has to be that it isn't
worth answering in detail, it's so transparently false."

"George," said Cornish, slowly.

"Yes?"

"Clapper did have and still has a bruise."

Gideon said: "Yes, and when the time comes we'll explain how he came by it. The best time will be when he's
up for his second hearing at the Magistrate's Court. We can
work it in then."

"All right," said Cornish. "Shall I tackle Clapper about
his posh friend?"

Gideon hesitated. He would have liked to talk to the
prisoner himself, but there was no real justification for inter-
vening. One of the big dangers of his job was the inclination
to feel that he alone could do everything best – Carson was
the latest victim of that kind of thinking. This was Cornish's
job; probably he would have been wiser to leave the questioning to Cornish yesterday.

"Yes, tackle him," Gideon decided at last.

"Want me to see the solicitor?"

"No," said Gideon. "If I'm right, Lewisham will let it all
soak in, and then make a formal protest at Bow Street on

Wednesday, during that second hearing. That's when we'll trot out the true version of what happened." Gideon frowned, pondering. "You know, we might be wiser to wait until then before we spring this 'posh voice' story. You'll have had time to dig a bit deeper, and we might even get a stronger lead. Follow all of Clapper's recent movements, find out everywhere he's been seen, check with all the Divisions, have a look round Mayfair." Gideon paused, and was oblivious of Matthew, standing to one side and listening intently. "Corny, I think that's the right angle. Ask all Divisions to check with all their men, uniformed and C.I.D. branch, and make up a detailed report on Clapper's movements. We've been working on anyone who saw him near the bank in Moorgate, and we've been concentrating on the East End because that's where he lives; this could put us on the beam. Will you fix it?"

"Glad to," said Cornish. "Then I'll get some sleep. Not worried about this *canard*, are you, George?"

"Wish it hadn't happened," Gideon said, "but no, I'm not worried about it." Yet as soon as Cornish had gone, he telephoned the police surgeon then on duty at the Yard, and after a brisk exchange, asked as if casually: "Didn't you once tell me that if a person's affected by something unpleasant – an ugly wound, a lot of blood, that kind of thing, he's likely to be affected whenever he comes up against it?"

"Yes," said the police surgeon. "I could show you a man who faints every time he cuts his finger. Why?"

"Just checking," said Gideon.

Then Kate came in and told him that she had arranged a family conference with the Mialls for next Wednesday evening. Why Wednesday, Gideon neither knew nor guessed. He thought that Kate made the announcement with a degree of satisfaction that was hardly justified, and which might mean that she and Mrs. Miall had worked out some way to help support two newly-weds while Matthew continued his studies. To Gideon, the idea was almost ludicrous, while there was a worrying factor, too. He and Kate were at last beginning to save a bit. If he had to start helping Matthew, Helen and a family, it would put a stop to savings. But he did not ask any questions, for he knew that Kate was trying to make sure that he did not have too much on his mind.

Because Monday was likely to be quite a day, too.

On Sunday night, Harrison watched his wife as she sat and watched television. Once or twice she yawned, and there were no indications that she would need a hot toddy or a capsule to make her sleep tonight. He had to be patient, but it was difficult – in fact it was almost impossible.

He kept picturing Chloe sitting where Pam was, now. The queer thing was that Chloe made up far more than Pamela, but too much lipstick and powder made Pam look like the tart. The silly bitch, nothing could make her look desirable; nothing in this world. The only desirable Pam was a dead one.

CHAPTER XII

FIRE FACTS

IN fact, Monday passed quietly for Gideon. The biggest 'new' job of the week-end was a cat burglar in Mayfair who raided three homes while the families were watching television, and got away with about nine thousand pounds' worth of jewellery. These, the smaller burglaries, the hold-ups, the hit and runs, the drunks, the vice cases, were simple routine. The Monday newspapers played down the story of Lewisham's accusation, and that was reassuring. Lewisham had been smart in selecting a Sunday newspaper which relied on sensation more than anything else; the move would almost certainly boomerang on him and on Clapper, and Gideon's preoccupation was to find out how to use it against Clapper.

At one o'clock, he left for the Eltham Cemetery, where a

crowd of nearly five hundred people stood about during the interment of the remains of the eight victims of the Lambeth fire. Television and movie cameras were in position, there were at least fifty reporters and some cameramen. A few of these took pictures of Gideon, but whenever he could he avoided them. He looked about the crowd, marvelling and feeling a little sick at the same time, for these were the gawpers. There were probably not more than a dozen mourners for the Miller family, no more than fifty or sixty for the Jarvises. The rest were the buzzards of a civilised city. He studied some of the faces, and among those he looked at was the pale, rather worried face of a small man, who was at the back of the crowd, and whose lips kept moving with the words of the Church of England parson who intoned at the graveside. Now and again, this man bowed his head. Gideon did not pay him serious attention, because he felt that the man was genuinely mourning, and that he might be a friend or a business acquaintance of the Millers. He gave Gideon the impression of being very humble, and after the ceremony he went slowly, perhaps sadly, towards the gates of the cemetery. Gideon saw him fasten cycle clips to his trousers, and then make off on a bicycle.

So did a dozen or so others.

Gideon saw Mrs. Jarvis and her eldest child, Hester, helped into a car by an elderly man, probably her father. This wasn't the time for him to talk to her, but he must make sure that she had all the help she needed. She looked pale and yet attractive in navy blue; the child had on obviously 'best' clothes and a black armband.

Gideon drove back to the Yard, and to nothing more exciting than an indecent exposure charge, from Piccadilly.

It was on the Wednesday afternoon that Lucky Margetson tapped at the door of his office, and when he came in, Gideon thought that he was looking mildly excited. Margetson reminded Gideon of a chunkier, plumper, slightly less irrepressible Lemaitre, and thinking of Lemaitre, he realised that there had been no word that the Ericsons or Roscoe had tried to get out of the country.

"What've you got, Lucky?" he inquired.

"Don't know that it's much," said Margetson, "but it's something we all ought to have got on to before, I do know that."

"What?"

"Every one of these five fires has taken place on a Wednesday night," Margetson announced, taking a slip of paper from his pocket. "The first Bethnal Green job was on Wednesday, December the 7th, the second —"

"I'll take your word for it," Gideon interrupted. "And it's Wednesday today." He felt a deep stirring of disquiet, and was about to give Margetson instructions to have all slum areas alerted, but stopped himself; it was better to let Lucky ask for what he wanted. "What do you make of it?" he demanded.

"Might be just a coincidence," Margetson said cautiously, "and the fires haven't been spaced out at regular intervals, either. But tonight might be the right time to have a special watch on all slum areas. Can't get that fact out of my mind – the fires were all in slum areas. I can't help feeling we might be looking for a looney."

Gideon thought, swiftly, sharply, of Mrs. Manson, and then held the thought. The fate of her daughter had driven the little woman mad, and she had set out to kill Briggs. Madness took different forms, remember. Margetson had spent a long time trying to find a motive for the fires, and hadn't succeeded, possibly because there wasn't one. There was no motive for madness, either, but there had to be a cause.

"Lucky," he said, "what would drive a man round the bend the way you think this man's gone?"

"Well, who knows?" asked Margetson. He was cautious to a fault, and in that regard a complete contrast to Lemaitre. "Some people are just born with it in them, as I was saying the other day about my own kid. I've been checking, George. We've had twenty-seven fire-raisers through our hands in the past eighteen months – London and Home Counties I mean – and seven of them have been remanded for medical attention, five of them are in one of

the mental hospitals. Taking those five – the ones even the
law agrees are round the bend – three of them are naturals,
a bit simple, and fire always excites them. Kind of primitive
fetishism, I suppose. One of them always set fire to the
home of someone who'd slighted him, a case of enemity suppressed too long before it burst out. The fifth one was badly
burnt in his childhood, and the psychiatrists said that it was
a way of getting his own back."

"Ah," said Gideon, softly.

"You there, too, are you?" asked Margetson, almost
lugubriously. "I suppose I ought to have expected it. What
we've got is a chap who starts a fire in some kind of slum on
a Wednesday, and as far as I can find out this crop of fires
started in Bethnal Green. But there wasn't any telephone
call reporting it. The man who raised the alarm was the
husband of the woman who was burned to death, with their
only child, a girl of eleven. You remember you asked me
about the burnt out car. It was this chap's. He was a tallyman named Biship – IP, not OP – who had a lot of East
London rounds, did a different round every day for two
weeks in a row, then started all over again. He can ride a
bike, and he measures up in size to the cyclist who rushed
off from Miller's place, after Jarvis shouted at him."

"Checked him?" demanded Gideon.

"He walked out of his job ten days after the fire," said
Margetson. "He'd been away for a week, on compassionate
leave, went back for three days, then threw his hand in. He
didn't tell anyone where he was going or what he was going
to do. He'd been out on the night of the fire – he had a
round out at Bromley which always kept him late, and this
was the day of that round. His firm hasn't heard from him
since. There's no funny business, no shortage in his accounts,
in fact a few quid commission is due to him. Practically
everything he possessed except the suit he had on and the
oddments in his case were destroyed in the fire, but he was
well insured. Collected a cool five thou'."

"Photograph?" asked Gideon.

"There's one of him in a group at a company outing, but
I don't think it will help much. I'm checking everyone who

knew him, trying to get a photo, but he had no close relations and no friends. The Biships were a cut above the
other people living in the neighbourhood, and didn't mix
with them much. He hadn't taken his car that day because
of a flat tyre, so he got back very late, walked the last two
miles to his home, and the fire was blazing when he got
there."

"We want him," Gideon declared. "Do everything necessary, and I'll sign any chits you need, or Joe will. Get busy,
Lucky."

"I couldn't be any busier," Margetson said, and hurried
out of the office. Before the door closed, Gideon called :

"Just a minute !"

The door clicked, Lucky disappeared, and a moment later
reappeared with his hand on the door.

"As it's Wednesday, tell Information to send a message
round to all East End – no, all Divisions – asking the men
on night beat duty to keep a special watch on all slum areas
on their beat," Gideon said. "You know what to tell them
to look for. Better advise them to pick up any cyclist they
don't know, or who can't explain what he's doing."

"Right !" Margetson hurried off again, and his footsteps
faded.

He had hardly gone before the telephone bell rang; this
time it was Cornish.

"Got a few minutes for me to go over tomorrow's case
against Clapper?" he asked.

"Yes, come round right away," said Gideon.

But the second hearing of the charge against Leonard
Clapper, he knew, would be important chiefly because of
the attitude of the solicitor, Lewisham. Cornish had made
no more progress with the man with the 'posh' voice, and it
might take weeks to find him. The inquest on Mrs. Clapper
had been adjourned for a week pending police inquiries;
there was no further progress on the case. Gideon discussed
every angle with Cornish, and the big superintendent was
about to leave when a telephone bell rang on Bell's desk.
Bell picked it up, and after a moment, said:

"Mrs. Gideon for you, George."

Gideon said: "Eh?" and looked astonished because Kate so seldom called when he was at the office, and inevitably when there was some kind of emergency. There was the coming family conference tonight, that was probably what she wanted to talk about. As he lifted his telephone, he thought with a grin that she was going to tell him to be home in good time, or else. "Hallo, Kate," he said, quietly, and Cornish went across to Bell's desk while Bell put down his receiver.

"Hallo, dear," said Kate speaking rather more quickly than usual. "I thought this would be worth a call. The conference is off this evening."

"Eh?"

"It's off, George, you needn't break your neck to get home."

"But why? What's happened?"

"The immediate crisis is over, you can say due to natural causes," Kate announced, and gave a little high-pitched laugh, which told more vividly than anything else could how she had felt about Matthew and Helen. "There's no need to worry, Helen will have a bad time for a day or two but she'll be all right."

"Well I'm damned," exclaimed Gideon. "Well, that takes the pressure off, somehow. All right, Kate. Tell you what, you come up to Town and we'll have a meal out somewhere. Haven't done that for months. Now, don't say you can't, I'll be free at six o'clock even if Joe Bell has to work overtime for the rest of the week ... Okay, dear, that's fine. I'm very glad." He rang off, grinned across at the others, said: "And you needn't look like that, this is my secret." He took out his pipe and began to fill it, then brought his mind to bear on his job. He simply hadn't time to think any more about Matthew, but he hadn't felt so easy in his mind for days.

One case before him was Riddell's, down at Brighton. Riddell seemed to be on top of the situation, and there was a lot to be said for the theory that if Chloe Duval was to be next on Harrison's list, there would be some sign of a cooling off in passion first. Better let the affair go on for a while.

Gideon did not give a thought to Harrison's wife. No one but Harrison did.

About that time the man whom Mrs. Tennison knew as Mr. Brown, and whose real name was Walter Biship, opened the door of Mrs. Tennison's kitchen apologetically, and said:

"I'm so sorry to worry you, Mrs. Tennison, but do you think I could have dinner a little earlier tonight? At half past six, say? I have to go out for the early evening, but I shall be home by ten o'clock."

"Couldn't be easier," declared Mrs. Tennison, "and it works out lovely, too, I can wash up and go to the pictures before the programme starts. Thank you *ever* so much."

"The question is, when are we going to do it, and how?" asked Ericson, late that same evening. "What scares me is that we're all followed, everywhere we go."

"I think the best thing would be to go and see that man from Scotland Yard," said Joan, quietly. "The man with the French name, Lemaitre. If you go there, surely it will tend to prove that you think you've nothing to fear."

"Could be," conceded Roscoe. "What can we offer?"

"We could buy back sixty-three per cent of the shares now," Ericson said, "and there's a reasonable chance that at least fifty per cent of the people who own them will think that we're really trying to buy back because we want to corner the market. We ought to be all right, provided the police —"

"What I need," said Roscoe, "is a stiff whisky."

Alan Paul Scarfe, *alias* Alan Peter Spender, *alias* Arthur Philip Simpson, sat in the Brighton flat, listening to television and reading at the same time. He still had the Sunday newspapers handy, and the *Globe* gave him especial pleasure. So did all mention of the allegations against Gideon. So far as he knew, the police were not yet on to him either as Scarfe or as Spender. Much would depend on what would happen at the second hearing tomorrow.

*   *   *

There was not a great deal that Biship had not learned about fires and their causes in the past five months, and he had learned that the simple way to start a fire was always the best. He was also a shrewd man, who knew quite well that once the police began to suspect the truth, the odds would be against him. Since he had recovered from the shock of the Miller tragedy, and since he had seen the tremendous amount of publicity which it had aroused, his mind had become very sharp indeed. The newspaper suggestion that the fires were connected told him that the police would be on the lookout in all slum areas, and there was another obvious fact: they would be on the lookout for a cyclist in the early hours of the morning. Moreover, the tragedy of the last fire had gained a lot of publicity and brought the problem of the slums into the open again. He felt as if he were really making progress. *And the landlords were the murderers.*

His work as a tallyman, first selling to housewives on the instalment system, and then visiting them once a fortnight to collect the payment on clothes and footwear, had taken him into most of the poorest and slummiest districts of London. Few men knew these districts better, few knew what areas of them ought to be destroyed. That evening, he hired a small car – having to pay a hundred pounds deposit – and spent a long time preparing some petrol soaked rags, and attaching to each a slow burning fuse made by soaking string in candle grease which he melted in an old saucer. He visited six different places that evening, just after dark, and made for little gloomy corners in smelly houses which looked liable to fall down. There was always plenty of rubbish to put near the pile, and once a fire started each place would burn like matchwood. He knew each district well, knew exactly how to get in and out of the various places, and hid whenever he heard footsteps near a place where he started a fire. He did everything with detached, business-like efficiency, and he was such a small and ordinary-looking man that no one took any notice of him.

The fuses gave off a slight smell and a wisp or so of smoke, but neither was so noticeable as a cigarette end smouldering, and the occupants of these homes were used to peculiar smells. Biship judged that the first fire would start at about half past ten, and the others would be staggered according to the length of fuses on them.

The last should begin about half past one.

He would be home and in bed soon after ten.

CHAPTER XIII

SMELL OF BURNING

"HALLO, Mum," said a bright-faced boy who lived near Lots Road Power Station, on the borders of Chelsea and Fulham. "I think I smell burning."

"It's only Mrs. Coker again, she's damped her fire down," his mother replied. "You put out that light and go to sleep."

"Okay, Mum." The boy stretched up in bed and touched the switch, for his bed – one of two in a room hardly large enough for one – was very close to the wall. Yet the wallpaper was attractive and newly put on by the boy and his father, while his mother had spent a lot of time making gay curtains and bedspreads. The two girls in the family slept on the double bed, divided from the boy's by a wooden screen also made by their father. The parents had a shake-down bed in the living-room. Every inch of space was utilised, and every inch was spotless.

The boy lay half asleep for a while, still vaguely aware of the burning, but quite reassured. His mother did not give the matter another thought. Nor did the two girls, who were going out for an hour, while the boy got to sleep. There was an absolute rule in this house that he be given no opportunity of peeping over or round the screen.

The smouldering was, in fact, behind a broken piece of wainscoting in an empty flat immediately beneath them.

Another family of five, who lived just across the river at Wandsworth in a hovel which was one of four hundred scheduled for demolition, presented a different kind of picture. They lived in and accepted squalor. The whole family slept in one room, the parents on a rickety double bed, the two daughters on narrow camp beds, the one boy, who was two years older than the girls, on the floor in a corner opposite the door. No one worried whether he 'peeped' or not. No one worried, in fact. The mother was a slattern who dreamed away half of her waking hours in the semi-stupor of the alcoholic, and the husband was a big, lusty and lustful man who took his pleasures wherever he could find them. The miracle was that the two girls always left their home and returned to it looking as if they had come out of a beauty parlour. They had one corner of the bedroom, with an orange box covered with chintz as a dressing-table, a mirror fastened to the wall, and their clothes in a corner hanging cupboard. In a casual, rather careless way, they were fond of their mother, who had one transcending gift: she could cook. Their father's good quality was that he always provided enough money. Out of doors, the whole family looked bright, fresh and healthy, except for the sleepy mother.

Gin had killed her sense of smell.

She and the sixth member of the family, a cat, were alone that evening in the living-room which was also the kitchen and washroom. She could not understand the cat, a tabby with a white patch over its right eye. It kept sniffing at the walls. This house was one of the few occupied here, the others were being emptied as new accommodation was found for the tenants.

The smell which worried the cat was next door.

There was a smell of burning in four other places; one at Bethnal Green not far from the scene of the first fire, another at Wapping, a third in Limehouse not far from the river, a fourth in Islington, quite near the spot where Briggs had made his ferocious and forlorn attempt to escape. In each case, someone sniffed and smelt burning, but in most cases this was put down to an everyday cause, because one stench or another was always likely to tease their sense of smell if not to offend it. Only one was investigated more thoroughly.

The first warning of fire reached the Chelsea Fire Station at half past eleven, when a horrified girl called 999, and explained breathlessly that she had just got home and found one of the rooms of her house on fire, and she couldn't make her mother hear. The engine was on the spot within three minutes, when smoke was already pouring out of the windows and there was a fierce red light shining on it, giving it an awful kind of beauty.

"I just opened the door, and there was a roar and everything caught fire," a girl sobbed. "I just opened the door, that's all I did."

"Is anyone in there?" asked a policeman who had rushed from the Police Station at the moment of the first warning.

"My Mum and my brother, they were inside. Oh, it's awful, it's awful," the girl kept sobbing, while her sister stood still and pale, dumbstruck. The father wasn't yet home from his working men's club.

The second alarm came from Wandsworth. Here, the fire-engines were on the scene very quickly, but the tinder-dry houses were catching alight one after the other, and it looked like being a big outbreak. Engines were summoned from Fulham, Clapham and soon from as far afield as Wimbledon. When the blaze was at its height, and while hundreds of people in their night clothes, clutching a few precious possessions, were being hustled out of the hovels, a third fire was reported at Wapping. Some of the East End Fire Service went out to that outbreak, and it proved to be much less dangerous, but a hundred houses were evacuated for safety's sake. By then, telephones were humming between Fire Stations and Divisional Police Headquarters and the Yard. It was a little after midnight when Gideon was called; Carmichael was on the other end of the line.

"I can't be sure that this is part of the other series," Carmichael said, "but there are three separate outbreaks, each with the same indications of arson, each in slum areas. The difference is that we had no mystery report of any of the fires. I am at the worst of them, in Wandsworth, and from the look of it I shall be here all night."

"As bad as that?" Gideon said heavily. He had been woken out of the first heavy sleep of the night, after the dinner with Kate.

"It is very bad indeed," answered Carmichael. "Just behind the section where the fire began there is an oil storage depot. If that catches, there will be a great deal of damage, as well as many casualties."

"I'll come over," Gideon said.

"I look forward to seeing you," declared Carmichael, as if they were talking about meeting for a drink. Gideon rang off, and hitched himself up on his pillows, yawned, and scratched his head. Kate was also hoisting herself up in bed.

"No, don't you get up," Gideon said. "There'll be a canteen over at Wandsworth, the mobile canteens always get out to these big shows." He realised that Kate didn't know what it was about. "'Nother big fire," he went on. "Wandsworth."

"Oh," said Kate. "George, I'll gladly make you —"

'Stay there," Gideon ordered, and smiled down at her. She had been happy during the evening, so relieved about Helen; Miall had said that the development made no difference to Matthew's duty to marry Helen. "But he agrees we can give ourselves time to think," Kate had said.

Nothing was more remote from Gideon now than Ted Miall. He dragged on his shirt and trousers, collected everything else he would need and went out, to finish dressing in the bathroom. He closed the door firmly on Kate. From the bathroom, he looked towards the river and beyond, and saw a red tinge in the sky in the direction of Wandsworth, a moving, flickering glow, not like that which came from neon lighting. He doused his face and hands in cold water, and by the time he went downstairs, was feeling much fresher. No one else stirred. He closed the door quietly, strode along

to the garage, and was startled when a figure emerged from
a doorway near it – a policeman about whom there was an
unmistakable odour of tobacco smoke.

"Good evening, sir."

"Just the man I need. Close my garage after me, will
you?" asked Gideon. "It's self-locking. Nasty fire over at
Wandsworth, I'm told."

"One of the series, sir?"

"Could be."

"Must say this," said the constable, a middle-aged man
not even slightly embarrassed at having been caught having
a smoke, "he only burns down the slummy stuff. If it wasn't
for the loss of life, you could almost say good riddance."

They stopped by the garage, and Gideon took out his
keys.

"Many people feel like that?" he asked.

"Oh, yes, sir. After all, in this day and age it's time such
things as slums were done away with, isn't it?"

"See what you mean," said Gideon. "Be a bit of an out-
cry if we cleared up all the slums before building new places
for people to live in, though."

"Oh yes, sir, but —"

He was the beat-lawyer, London's equivalent to the sea-
lawyer, and at any other time Gideon would have been
sharp about the smoking. Now, he was anxious to get on
the way, and was very thoughtful. This man had simply
put into words what Carmichael and Margetson had said
and he had thought; there was a great deal of sympathy for
what was going on. But for that hideous blaze when eight
had died – that was understandable.

Would there be any casualties tonight? Would the firemen get this blaze under control before it set off an explosion
at that oil storage plant?

Gideon knew the place, some distance away from the
main road but on the river and with a slum area quite near
it. There must be a dozen storage tanks inside the steel
mesh protected walls, for this depot fed a large section of
London with its fuel. Gideon drove fast, crossing Putney
Bridge, then winging left off the High Street and heading

for Wandsworth that way. Now and again, at the end of a long street or when this road went straight ahead, he could see the deepening red glow in the sky, and he began to doubt whether Carmichael's men could keep this under control. He found himself watching the sky, fearful in case it was suddenly split by the explosive glare that would tell of an explosion.

He saw a man step off the pavement straight in front of him, jammed on his brakes, knew a moment of wild dread – and came to a standstill only a few yards away from the man, who was wearing a policeman's uniform. He came slowly and purposefully to Gideon's window, and as Gideon opened it, he said:

"Excuse me, sir, you're going a bit fast even for one o'clock in the morning, aren't you? May I see your licence, please?" He thrust his head inside the car, and Gideon knew that he was sniffing and expecting to smell alcohol on the driver's breath. Gideon took out his driving licence, always handy for identification, and handed it over.

"Next time don't step out so suddenly," he said. "It would have been as much your fault as mine if I'd knocked you down."

"You were going too fast, sir, and – *Mr. Gideon!*"

"On my way to that fire," Gideon said. "But you're right, I must have been doing sixty."

"As it's official business, sir, that's quite all right." The man was badly shaken. "Very nasty fire, I'm told. I saw my sergeant ten minutes ago, and he said that he didn't think they would be able to save —"

The booming roar of the explosion burst upon his words.

CHAPTER XIV

LETTERS

GIDEON just heard the roar.

Carmichael and Margetson, sheltering behind a cement building which would stand up to almost any blast, were deafened by the explosion. Within sight, fifty or sixty policemen and firemen were driving back the crowd, as they had been driving them back for the last fifteen minutes. In the red glow of the inferno, the sweating faces of the firemen and the policemen, the snaking hoses, the great hissing jets of water, the great clouds of smoke, all turned the quiet of the night into a holocaust. As the first explosion came, two men were blown off their feet and but for the efforts of the police, another fifty would have been. A fireman atop a swaying escape and directing a stream of water towards some of the storage tanks which were not yet affected, was blown back; the nozzle was snatched out of his hand. He stood swaying wildly on the edge of the platform, while a man just below strove desperately to save him.

Another tank exploded with a menacing, booming roar, the air in and above the depot seemed to become a seething, writhing mass of metal and burning debris. Margetson, staring at the struggling man on the escape, saw him falling, saw the six men beneath him making last minute and almost despairing efforts to spread the net.

They caught him.

More fire engines were coming, alarms rang continuously, and heavy police reinforcements were drafted into the area as more and more homes were threatened. Debris from the explosion, hurled hundreds of feet into the air, fell upon the little houses, upon shops and offices, upon larger houses; some wasted themselves in the river and hissed and seethed angrily; some fell sullenly on waste ground.

Gideon, stopped nearly half a mile away from the scene, saw much of this as he turned the corner. A constable told him where to find Carmichael. Heat from the fires and red light which was everywhere fell upon his face, and lit up the whole district with its devilish glow. Gideon didn't run, but strode as fast as his strong legs would carry him, desperately anxious to find out what the casualties were likely to be. He heard the ting-a-ling-ting of an ambulance, and was pushed to one side as it moved along. In the distance other ambulance bells were ringing.

He was forced to stop at a corner where a police radio car was parked. Round the corner was a police crowd-control car, its loud speaker silent for the moment. An ambulance swung round the corner, and as it passed Gideon heard a man call from the police car:

"There's another one."

"Another what?" a man called back.

"Another bloody fire! Out at Limehouse, this time, got a whole block of tenements."

Gideon strode to the car. "I'm Gideon," he announced. "What's this about a fire at Limehouse?"

"Just had it over the air, sir," a man said. "Big show, too. That's five tonight."

"Five?"

"One at Bethnal Green, one at Lots Road, this one, and one at Wapping."

"I see," said Gideon. "How many control cars further up?"

"This is the advance one, sir."

"Check on the other fires and send reports up to me every fifteen minutes," said Gideon. "Tell Information to call Mr. Rogerson, and advise him of the situation, also advise him I don't think it will help if he comes out, but if he does it might be better for him to go to the next largest fire."

"Very good, sir."

"Know if Mr. Margetson is here?"

"Saw him with Mr. Carmichael half an hour ago, sir."

"Thanks," said Gideon. He went striding off, feeling the heat getting worse, his anxiety greater, his face brushed every now and again with hot smuts, his mind depressed under the weight of dread. He heard the hissing of water, steam and fire. He reached a small concrete wall, and found Margetson and Carmichael standing in front of it. An ambulance was moving away.

"What kind of casualty list?" demanded Gideon.

Margetson jumped round. "Hallo, sir!"

"Good evening, Gideon," said Carmichael. "It is impossible to be sure, but largely due to the promptness with which your people worked, I think most of the district was cleared. Casualties should be limited to my men and yours – except for two in the house where fire was first found. I was told only ten minutes ago that it started in a house next to one where they've been keeping paint ready for some decorating work, a kind of estate paint store. Once that caught alight —" He broke off, as the ambulance passed, and then said: "I think we're over the worst, now."

"Here, anyhow," Gideon said. "Lucky, there's another, at Limehouse."

"Gawd," breathed Margetson. "Five of them in one flickin' night. It can't be a coincidence. This time there weren't any telephone calls, though." He looked at Carmichael. "Need me here, Mr. Carmichael? I ought to go and take a peek at all the others."

"Please proceed," said Carmichael. The burnishing light of the fire made him seem very handsome, and he had not looked away from the flames all the time that Gideon had been here. "I am still sure that we're over the worst here." He broke off as a fire officer came up, saluted, and said:

"We're on top of it in the petrol depot, sir, and that means we're over the worst."

"How's that man who fell just now?"

"Not serious, sir, apart from a broken leg. But one of our chaps has got his, I'm afraid – caught by a chunk of metal as big as the side of a house."

Carmichael said: "Oh," and made no other comment.

"Come on," Gideon said to Margetson. "I'll be seeing you, Carmichael."

*   *   *

There were not only the fires to worry about; there were the sneak-thieves and the looters. The police automatically watched for these and went into action against them. A middle-aged policeman in the Limehouse district, NE Division, was hurrying towards the scene of the fire there when he saw a movement inside a shop where the roof was smouldering, and giving off occasional flames. He stood to one side, and watched a very big man shoulder his way out of a doorway into the shop.

"There's Tiny Repp," the policeman said with satisfaction, and looked round for help. A police car was turning the corner, and he waved it down. As it drew up, the shop door opened and the giant appeared in it. At sight of the car and the policeman he drew back.

"So you couldn't miss a chance, Tiny," the policeman said. "This will send you down for three years. When are you going to learn?"

"B-b-but I wasn't doing anything!" the giant protested. "I thought old Gran Muggs was upstairs, I didn't want her to burn to death. I thought —"

"You thought there were some easy pickings," jeered one of the men from the car. "Don't make a fuss, Tiny. Come along."

"But —" the big man began, and then gulped and fell silent.

The fire at Wandsworth was the worst.

Gideon and Margetson, in Gideon's car, went from fire to fire, took on-the-spot reports, and began to form a picture of how they had started. The timing had been remarkable – each had been within about half an hour of the previous outburst, and there seemed little doubt that there was a deliberate rhythm in that. A smaller fire, at Islington, had been discovered, with the remains of a loose ball of petrol soaked rag, not much bigger than a cricket ball, which had been found with the ash of a fuse close to it. Had the occupant of the house not smelt burning and sent for the fire brigade, it would have developed into another inferno.

At half past five, Gideon and Margetson headed for the

Yard, faces blackened, clothes singed in places, Hallowe'en masks of men, their red-rimmed and tired eyes reflecting the horror of all they had seen.

"No point in going back home," Gideon said to Margetson. "We'll have a snack and a shower here, and I'll put my head down for a couple of hours. You'd better, too."

Margetson said: "Don't know that I feel like taking any time off until we've found this chap." Nine out of ten Yard men would have said 'this swine' or 'this devil' or something stronger. "I'm going to be on the ball by ar' past eight. We've got to find that tallyman, Biship, even if it means knocking on every door throughout the whole perishing area."

Gideon said, heavily: "There are nearly two million front doors in London."

"We've got a week, anyhow, I'd say," said Margetson. "Every Wednesday —"

"Hold it," said Gideon, and after Margetson had paused, he went on : "Until tonight, there was one fire at a time. Until tonight, there was always plenty of warning to allow people to get away. If this was the same chap, then he changed his tactics because of the publicity he got on Sunday and last week. He knows we're looking for a cyclist. He knows we've got a description. He knows that we are putting two and two together. If he changed his tactics tonight, he might well change them again – by selecting a different night, say. We can't wait until next Wednesday. We've got to get the door-to-door laid on, and we've got to get thousands of the photograph from that group printed. Even when we've done it," he added, "we can't be sure that Biship's our man."

Margetson didn't speak.

Gideon had a sandwich and some tea, a shower and a shave with the electric razor he kept at the office, then went to the rest room on the top floor, where there were a dozen camp beds for emergency use. Two men were sleeping there already, one of them snoring. There was no sign of Margetson. Gideon took off his shoes, loosened his collar and lay down. The rhythmic snoring began to irritate him, but soon he got used to it, and his eyes began to close. He

couldn't have had an hour's sleep at home. That fact and
the surfeit of fires seemed to dull his senses. He kept dozing,
then reminded himself that by the time the night's toll was
reckoned there might be a dozen fatalities, and might be
even more. Until a few days ago they had not even begun
to suspect that there was a kind of chain reaction behind
the slum fires, but now – God, why hadn't *he* cottoned on
to it sooner?

He felt a hand on his shoulder, shaking him. He started,
woke, opened his eyes, and saw Lemaitre bending over him,
this morning wearing a plain mauve tie and a brown suit
much too gingery for first thing in the morning. Someone
else was in the background. Lemaitre was holding a newspaper in his right hand and shaking Gideon with his left.
He stopped, said: "Show a leg, George, for Gawd's sake."
The other figure materialised into a uniformed constable
carrying a cup of tea. The steam rising from it showed
misty and mysterious against the bright sunlight at a
window. Sunlight!

Gideon sat up.

"'Morning, Lem," he said, and glanced at his watch; it
was only a quarter past eight. "Gimme." He took the tea.
"What woke you up?"

"What woke me is going to wake you," Lemaitre said,
with tension shrill in his voice, "and I don't mean the
Ericsons, either, that's small beer compared with this.
Look." He thrust the newspaper towards Gideon, and
nothing would ever stop him from behaving like an over-
grown school-boy.

Gideon read:

RECORD GETS LETTER FROM FIRE-RAISER

Intends to Burn Down All Slums

Gideon hadn't yet sipped his tea; and his hand did not
move.

"They all got one," Lemaitre said. "Every newspaper

out this morning got it, George. Three of them stopped printing so as to change the headlines. They all telephoned here, your desk looks like a mountain already. They —"

Gideon began to sip his tea.

"What've you done?" he demanded, between sips.

"Eh?"

"Don't stand there saying 'eh'. What've you done?"

"*I*'ve only just got in, I —"

"Priddy was on duty last night – what's he done?" Gideon began to get off the bed, keeping the cup level all the time, sipping again two or three times, making a tremendous effort to appear composed. "Talked to him?"

"Just had a word —"

"Get him on the phone."

"Okay, George," Lemaitre said, in a more subdued tone, and stretched out for the telephone. Gideon finished his tea, tied the laces of his shoes, and then Lemaitre held out the telephone. Gideon took it, and leaned against the wall.

"Priddy?"

"Yes, George."

"What've you done about those letters?"

"Send round for each of them, three are in already," said Priddy. "There were eight altogether – six morning dailies, two evenings. The letter's identical in each case. Typewritten – some are carbon copies. Not yet sure what the machine is, but I think it's a fairly old Olivetti portable, the very light kind. Want me to read one?"

"How long is it?"

"Better part of a page."

"See they're all on my desk, will you?" asked Gideon, "and tell me the drift."

"It's in the headlines. This chap says that slums are a blot on the face of London, and that as the authorities have left them standing for so long, he's going to destroy them all. What this city needs, he says, is another Great Fire of London before the authorities will sit up and take notice. Cracked, of course."

Gideon didn't answer.

"You there, George?" asked Priddy.

"Yes," said Gideon. "Thanks. I'll be in my office in about twenty minutes. Any idea where Margetson is?"

"No. Last time I saw him, he said he was going to check on a few odds and ends."

"Try and find him, I want to see him," Gideon said, and then asked the question which almost frightened him. "What was the total casualty list last night?"

"Not too bad, all things considered," Priddy said, almost brightly; he was showing now what Gideon had always believed, that he was a man with little or no imagination. "Six dead, twenty-one injured, only three of them seriously. There were two firemen among the dead and seven among the injured. Four of our chaps injured. The other dead were in two houses at the heart of the fire – mother and a boy of eleven at Lots Road, a mother and one girl at Wandsworth."

"Hmm," said Gideon. "Could be worse, I suppose." He grated the words out, added: "Ta," and rang off. He poked his fingers through his wiry hair, then lifted the telephone. "Telephone my wife," he ordered. "Tell her I slept at the Yard and won't be home until this evening, possibly late – got that?"

"Yes, sir."

"Get Mr. Carmichael, the Chief Fire Officer for London on the line for me in my office at nine o'clock sharp. Put through any official who calls about the fire. If Mr. Margetson calls, I'll talk to him. Check with me before any other calls are put through."

"Yes, sir."

"Right." Gideon banged the receiver down, went into the cloak-room and sluiced his hands and face with cold water again, and said to the constable: "Go down to the canteen, get me some bacon and eggs and the trimmings, toast, butter and sweet marmalade, and some tea." He glanced at Lemaitre. "You had breakfast?"

"Yes, but I wouldn't mind a cuppa."

"Tea for two," Gideon said. "Come on, Lem." He let the uniformed man go out first, and went downstairs in the lift and straight along to the office of the Back Room inspector, the man who served the Press with statements about current cases and investigations. A sergeant was on duty, the C.I. in charge hadn't arrived. "Soames, tell anyone who comes in that we want —"

The door which led from the Embankment opened, and a newspaperman put his head into the room, tired-looking, unshaven and gaunt; he must have been on duty all night. He gave a curious kind of whoop, and pushed further in, letting the door slam behind him.

"Just right timing, Commander!" he greeted. "I'm from the *Daily Globe*. I wonder if —"

"I've got a statement for everyone outside," Gideon said, and had hardly finished before there was a tap at the door and five men came through in a bunch, one of them even dirtier and more tired-looking than the first, the others spruce after a night's sleep.

"Hold it," Gideon said, as two of them started to ask questions. "Here's a statement about last night's fires. We have reason to believe that they were started by a man driven insane by grievous personal loss in a previous fire. We have been looking for such a man for several days. We would like to interview a Mr. Walter Biship – IP, not OP – a tallyman or door-to-door salesman for the clothing and footwear firm of Smith, Wiseman and Griggson, of Shoreditch, and Mr. Biship may be able to give us some information."

He paused.

"Biship your man?" asked a young reporter.

"I'll tell you when we've talked to him. We would also like a recent photograph of him from any friend or relation who may have one, the only one we have at the moment is taken from an old group photograph and he doesn't show up very well. That's all about Biship." The men were scribbling furiously. "There were twenty-six casualties last night . . ."

When he had finished, and the men had gone, the Chief Inspector on duty by day came in, an elderly man who had been at the door for the last few minutes.

"Thanks, Commander," he said. "I hoped you'd keep

'em at bay for a bit. How much am I to tell them when they come back?"

"Release any news you get about the fire unless I tell you to hold it," Gideon said, and added almost under his breath: "He says he thinks we need a new Fire of London, and if he goes on at this rate he'll start one. Don't tell the Press I said that, mind."

CHAPTER XV
DOOR-TO-DOOR

GIDEON hesitated with a hand on the door of his office. It was still only twenty minutes to nine, and he felt as if he had been up all day. His eyes were bleary and stinging, and one of them kept itching. Bell wouldn't be here yet, and Margetson had gone off. There would be the morning's routine to get through, and although he could leave some of that to Bell when his *aide* came in, he could not push everything on to the older man. He knew even before he opened that door that it was going to be a difficult day, and he paused to take a deep breath, actually a deep physical breath, and to remind himself that at all costs he must prevent the night of fires from making him lose his sense of perspective and his balance.

He pushed open the door.

Joe Bell looked up from his desk, apparently no more tired than usual, coat off already, collar a little frayed at the edges. Margetson sat at a corner of the same desk, with a telephone at his ear. He started to get up.

"Siddown," Gideon ordered, and his heart lifted. "'Morning, Joe. What brought you?"

"Heard about the fires on the seven o'clock news, and I thought I'd better get a move on," Bell said. "Wish you'd called me."

"Someone had to keep awake today," Gideon said.

"While I think of it, lay someone on to telephone me the moment they know what time Clapper's up for that second hearing, I want to be there."

"George, why don't —"

"I'm going to be there, Joe. If I'm not they'll say I'm dodging the assault issue."

"I'll fix it," Bell said.

"You sure?" Margetson said into the telephone. "Eh? . . . Yes, okay . . . Yes, absolute priority, Commander Gideon . . . right, thanks." He rang off. Unlike Gideon, he hadn't shaved, his chunky face with its deep grooves gave the impression that he was trying to grow a beard. One of his eyes was very bloodshot, and there was a little angry burn scar near it, red and sore. His hair was singed on one side. "'Morning, George," he said.

"Hallo, Lucky. Who was that?"

"I've been on to the superintendent of seven of the Divisions, all those on the north-east, north-west, north and central," Margetson said, "and I've laid on the door-to-door search for Biship. Had one bit of luck already."

"What's that?"

"A photograph's turned up, and not a bad one either. We dug up some relations of Biship's yesterday, out at Penge, and they've sent the photo. It was on my desk when I got in. I've sent it through to Photographs, and they're sending a print over to the Repro. Agency. I've ordered five thousand."

"When for?"

"Midday today."

A smile began to ease the tension at Gideon's mouth, and he looked at Bell.

"This chap will make quite a copper when he's learned to get a move on, won't he?" he said. "What happened during the night, Joe?"

"Guess," said Bell, and there was an edge of disgust in his voice.

"The rats were out."

"The rats were out," Bell agreed. "There were twenty-seven cases of burglary in the Wandsworth area, fifteen in

Chelsea, every damned place where we had a fire the rats came out like a plague. We've picked up about half of them. Nine cases of looting were reported from shops and burned houses, and we caught two of the looters. Funny thing, there weren't any big jobs."

"Thanks be for small mercies," Gideon said, and jerked his tie loose as he dropped into his chair. "Got all the fires down on the reports, Lucky?"

"Yes. The desk tells me you've got a call in to Carmichael at nine o'clock, so I thought I'd better wait."

"Why don't you go and —"

"I've had all the breakfast I want," said Margetson, "but what I would like is to go round to all the Divisions and make sure they're lined up for the door-to-door hunt for Biship." There was the fervour of dedication in Margetson's voice, and he got up and studied the map of the Metropolitan Police District, hanging on a wall at one side of Gideon's desk. Gideon got up, too, and Bell joined them. "Could be wrong, but this chap must have gone round to all six places sometime yesterday evening, laying the fires on somehow. The fires were in AB, ST, QR, NE and KL. That's a hell of a wide area. He could have come into the area from one of the outer Divisions, but remember he's been seen using a bicycle, and you don't usually cycle a long distance especially if you're in a hurry. We can be sure this chap always knew he might be in a hurry. So I've been on to all the central Divisions, but —"

Gideon said: "You go and get a car and a driver, you don't want to have to drive yourself. See all the central Divisional chaps yourself, say I've sent you, say I'm flaming mad. I'll telephone each one of them and tell 'em you're on the way. I'll get Joe to telephone the outer Divisions, too, and in case we can't fix that right away, we'll send out a teleprint message to them. We'll ask for —" he paused, and frowned as he went on: "We'll tell them to draft half of their available men, uniformed and C.I.D. to help in the neighbouring central Divisions. You get the Divisions to carve their manors up so that we can get as many houses called as possible before the day's out. Don't wait for photographs but start pushing them out as soon as some are available – everyone's got a copy of Biship's description by now, that'll be good enough to start on. I'll keep you posted with anything Carmichael says or anything that turns up."

Margetson was already by the door.

"Thanks, George," he said almost humbly.

"And get yourself a square meal," Gideon said roughly. "Won't help if you starve yourself. There's one other thing, Lucky."

"Yes."

"We might not get him," Gideon reasoned, grimly. "He might decide that last night was such a success that he'll have another go tonight. He might also decide that as the Wandsworth petrol dump was his real winner, petrol dumps and places where fire will spread quickly are what he wants. So as you go round, make sure that all danger spots of that kind have special protection. I'll send a teleprint message out on it, you rub it in."

"I'll rub it it," Margetson assured him.

"And keep plugging at one other thing," Gideon went on, without adding that this was the one which haunted him. "Try to think *how* he'll strike next. If we can out-think him, we might stop him next time. If he out-thinks us, I wouldn't like to say what will happen."

"George, he can't get away now," Joe Bell was stung to say.

"If this chap was sane, I'd agree with you," Gideon said. "If he's not, he's only got to go round tonight with a dozen little *billets doux* containing a core of nitro-glycerine or even TNT, and in a couple of hours he could start a hell of a lot."

"I get it," Margetson commented, with the door half open. "We'll out-think him." He went out, while Bell sat at his desk, obviously badly shaken.

"I suppose you're right," he said uneasily.

"If I'm only half right it'll be bad enough," Gideon said. "Where's that letter he sent to —"

A telephone rang on his desk. He stared at it, and then said: "I'll take this one, but remind the exchange to get all the calls vetted this morning before they're put through to us. Then send for Lemaitre, he went back to his office to check some figures." He lifted the receiver. "Gideon . . . Who? . . . Oh, all right." He covered the mouthpiece with his great hand. "Riddell, I might switch him over to you." Obviously he was not going to have any time wasted by Riddell. 'Yes, Rid, but keep it short, I —"

"I won't keep you long, I can read the newspapers," Riddell interrupted, and there was a note of real satisfaction in his voice. "Just thought you'd like your mind relieved on one case, George."

"You got Harrison?"

"Near as dammit, I've got Harrison," Riddell crowed. "The hammer toe did it. There were five similar operations in Brighton about the time this dead woman had hers – they reckon she's twenty-four or-five, and was about ten when she had the operation. Four of the women are married and all alive-o, the fifth disappeared two years ago. She was supposed to be emigrating to Australia. Want to know something, George?"

"She knew Harrison."

"She and Harrison had quite an affaire," answered Riddell, with that same crowing note in his voice. "And that's not all, I think we've identified the second girl, from a dental job. The chap who did it retired and went to live in Devon, but the dental mechanic who worked for him still works for his successor, and recognised some bridge work. The retired dentist came up from Devon yesterday afternoon, and tells me it's certainly work he did on a Maggie Mason's mouth, three years ago. He remembers Maggie Mason, she was quite a floosie. And Maggie and Harrison had themselves quite a time, too. She disappeared – went to London to get married, it was said. We've got him, George. Shall I bring him in?"

Gideon said: "Get all the evidence checked, get the depositions ready, make sure that Harrison can't leave Brighton and make sure that he doesn't have a chance of taking this Chloe Duval where he can do away with her quietly. Then if you satisfied, send for Harrison and talk to him."

"That's my baby!" Riddell said. "Thanks, George." He had never 'Georged' Gideon before. 'I won't worry you unless I have to."

A telephone was ringing on Bell's desk while Bell was talking to someone else on the house phone.

"Thanks," said Gideon. "Be a nice clean job, Rid." He rang off, paused only for a moment, felt relieved that action would soon be taken against Harrison; it would be hellish if this Duval woman was killed before the police acted.

Well, he needn't worry about it now.

He saw Bell put one receiver down and pick up the other. He listened, and looked at Gideon. "Carmichael," he mouthed. "I'll take it," said Gideon, and picked up his receiver and then pressed a bell push on his desk, for a messenger. He gave no more thought to Brighton, not even a fragmentary one to Harrison's wife. "Hallo, Carmichael, sorry to worry you so early, but I'm wondering if you've any reports on the causes of the fires yet?"

Carmichael answered quietly and promptly: "Yes, on four of them. The ash of petrol soaked rags was found in hiding places difficult to get at, and so placed that in three cases the whole ball of ash remained in shape, in the other it had fallen to pieces. Other ash near the rag-ash shows that wood, cardboard or paper and some unidentified material burned close to the rags, suggesting that material which would catch fire quickly was stacked round the rags. In each case there was a trail of slow burning fuse —"

"Can you say what kind?"

"I would say that it was a home-made fuse made of tallow soaked string," said Carmichael, "but it may be some time before we can be sure. We can be positive that it was arson in each of the four cases. In two others, the indications are that the cause was the same but we may never be able to say for certain, there was too much damage at the seat of the fire."

"Hmm. Anything else?"

"I've no more information," Carmichael said, in his rather aloof voice. "But I am badly worried."

"About his next move?"

"Yes."

"I can imagine," Gideon said. "I've been telling Margetson, we've got to out-think —"

"How can you out-think a madman?" demanded Carmichael, and for once there was some heat and feeling in his voice. When Gideon didn't answer, he went on more quietly: "I am quite aware that we have to try, but I feel the best chance we have is finding out who it is and stopping him before he can try again. The success of last night's fire at Wandsworth might possibly give him more ambitious ideas."

"Yes, we'd got round to that," said Gideon, heavily. "We'll give it all we've got. I've arranged . . ." He told Carmichael what he proposed to do, and was still talking to the Chief Fire Officer when the door opened and Lemaitre came in, followed by a messenger. "Yes, we'll tell you the moment we get any news," Gideon promised, and rang off. He sat back in his chair, looked at the messenger with a frown, and lifted a finger at Lemaitre, enjoining silence. "Now why did I send – oh, I know. Telephone the North London Hospital, ask how Mr. Carson is, and put a written message about it on my desk. Also, telephone Mr. Manning of QR, apologise that I can't call myself, ask if he'll be good enough to find out if there is anything we can do for Mrs. Jarvis."

"The widow of Police Constable Jarvis, sir?" The messenger was an old policeman with a subdued manner.

"Yes."

"Very good, sir." The man went out, and as the door closed, Gideon looked at Lemaitre, and asked with hardly a moment's pause : "Lem, apart from the Ericson job, what've you got on hand?"

"Nothing that can't wait."

"Stand in for Joe and me with the briefing, then, will you? I don't want to cancel the session, and you'll know what's what in most cases. Use Rogerson's outer office, he won't be in until twelve." He touched a note on his desk. "He was at the Lots Road fire last night, didn't get home until seven o'clock."

"Poor old lad," scoffed Lemaitre. "I'll fix it, George."

"The Ericsons flown yet?"

"Can't make them out at all," said Lemaitre, as if annoyed as well as puzzled. "Roscoe is still staying at their place out at Esher, they don't show any signs of packing up and leaving. But I'll get them somehow or other, don't you worry. Shall I send to you if I can't cope with a job?"

"Yes. Warn anyone who comes I may have to keep 'em waiting."

"Right," said Lemaitre. "I'll keep 'em away if I can, but I did hear that Cornish wanted to have a word."

Gideon nodded as a telephone bell rang, and was poised ready to answer. He had never felt more conscious of his responsibility and the danger of not being able to meet it.

This was the call to MX Division, and he talked immediately to the Chief Superintendent in charge, laid everything on, added that Margetson would soon be at the Divisional Headquarters, and rang off. He talked to five other Divisional chiefs, all in the space of fifteen minutes, wasting hardly a word with any of them; only one man started to talk about other problems than the fire. Then Gideon spoke to NE Division, the toughest Division in the area; the brisk Chief Superintendent Hopkinson, the recently appointed Divisional Superintendent, had a laugh in his voice when he said:

"I thought you'd soon be on, George. Margetson's sitting opposite me now. The answers are yes, yes, yes, it's all laid on."

"Good," said Gideon. "Make a real job of it, Hoppy. No slap-stick."

Hopkinson chuckled.

"I've got one bit for you, George. Spare a minute?"

"Half a minute," conceded Gideon.

"Remember Tiny Repp?" asked Hopkinson, and Gideon wished that he wouldn't choose this moment to tell what was obviously going to be one of his anecdotes about the remarkable behaviour of old lags in his manor. Tiny Repp was a man no one was ever likely to forget, for he was perhaps the biggest burglar and breaking-and-entering specialist known to the Yard. Most burglars were on the small side; Tiny Repp was even bigger than Gideon, but had a remarkable facility for getting through small spaces, because he was double-jointed. He had been inside on four different occasions, but Gideon did not think he had been up for trial for several years; it was always a pity when an old lag who had made an effort to go straight fell down again.

"Yes, I know, but —"

"We caught him red-handed in a shop near the Wapping fire," Hopkinson said. "Know what he wanted us to believe?"

"Try me."

"Says that he thought the old girl who runs the shop was upstairs, and as the roof was on fire he went in to try to save her."

"Was she there?"

"She's been sleeping next door for days! He knew it all right, too."

"Not necessarily," said Gideon, doubtfully.

"Now, listen, George —"

"Tiny's been out of trouble for so long I don't want to think he's back into it," said Gideon. "Have you charged him?"

"Not formally. There's a lot doing this morning, I was holding him until later and going to charge him so that he comes up tomorrow."

"Give him a break," Gideon urged. "Let him go home, and tell him you're looking for evidence. Then see how he reacts when you bring him in again."

"Soft-hearted, aren't you?" Hopkinson jeered, but he laughed. "All right, George, one thing's certain. He won't run away."

Gideon said: "Thanks, Hoppy." He rang off, and sat back for a few seconds, and while he was sitting there, thought about Tiny Repp, keeping the bigger issues away, as small things often did. He wondered if he had been wise to interfere in what was really the trivia of the Division's work, and he was telling himself that it didn't really matter when there was a tap at the door. The messenger he had sent out earlier came in, carrying several photographs.

"What is it?" Gideon asked.

"I've come to report as instructed, sir," the man said in a slow, witness-box voice. His expression did not change. "Mr. Carson's leaving hospital this afternoon, sir, his condition is much improved. Mrs. Jarvis does not require anything at the moment, a sister from the country is staying with her, and will be in attendance for several weeks. Mr. Manning is of the opinion that everything will work out all right with the widow. In addition, sir, these photographic prints have just come in." He handed the photographs to Gideon, six of the same one – of little Walter Biship, showing him as rather shy-looking, the quiet type, not outstanding in any way, the kind of face which seemed to belong to a lot of different people. Gideon had a feeling that he had seen the man before.

"All right, thanks," he said, and as the constable marched out he flicked one of the photographs over to Bell. Neither of them spoke, but each man had a mental picture, of hundreds upon hundreds of policemen and detectives going systematically through the streets of London, the narrow streets and the wide ones, the streets with hovels and the streets with tall buildings, the block of flats and the better residential areas, the tenement blocks in the poor ones. Men would be going into the little shops, the pubs, the barbers, the little hotels and the doss-houses, and all the time Biship was somewhere in hiding, or at least unknown – somewhere thinking up his next move with the tortuous cunning of the man whose mind was unhinged.

Gideon seemed to hear the tramp of feet, to hear the banging on knockers, to hear the ringing of bells, to see the countless surprised glances, the people staring at the photographs, the shaking heads.

"No, no, no, no."

But Biship must be somewhere in London.

*   *   *

Biship was in his bed-sitting-room at Mrs. Tennison's, listening to the half past ten news headlines. His eyes were glittering. His lips were working. He kept nodding his head vigorously. He winced when the announcer said :

"Scotland Yard is organising a door-to-door search for Walter Biship who it is believed can give the information which may help in identifying the man who started last night's widespread fires."

On the small table in 'Mr. Brown's' room was a little Olivetti typewriter, and covering this were three newspapers, bought at different shops so that he should not arouse any comment for buying more than his usual number. Each of these had headlines about his letter; two of them had reproduced it, in the same size of the actual type.

"It's going to work," Biship breathed. "They're going to have to do something now. I want just one more big demonstration – one big fire, one really big fire."

His eyes were glassy with excitement, and he spluttered as he spoke.

Then he said : "If I could only get some nitro-glycerine, or some TNT. If I could only get some . . ."

He stopped abruptly.

He remembered the headquarters and storage yard of a quarrying firm in Lambeth, where he called once a fortnight to collect instalments from the thirty odd employees, and collected fresh orders, too. If he showed himself there he would be recognised, of course, but he had been going in and out of the place for years, he knew it almost as well as people who worked there knew it; he could find the back way in. In a locked cement storehouse, stacks of dynamite and smaller supplies of nitro-glycerine were kept, for quarry blasting jobs out in the country.

Biship began to recall everything he knew of this place.

That was the very instant when a telephone bell rang on Gideon's desk, and he was told :

"Clapper will be in the dock in about twenty minutes, sir."

That was also the very minute when Harrison was saying

to himself: "I can't wait any longer. She's got to go to-night."

By some ironic twist of events, Pamela was sleeping rather better, and feeling better in herself, so she didn't need hot toddy to get to sleep. Harrison couldn't know that her calmer mood was due to her new-found confidence in the expensive make-up, and her new hairdresser. Nor did he dream that because he watched her so closely, wanting her to droop, she believed he was taking more notice of her.

She was very nearly happy.

CHAPTER XVI

SECOND HEARING

GIDEON entered the Police Court a minute before Leonard Clapper was brought in through the door from the cells. The sergeant-in-charge came first, and two constables followed Clapper, who was big and still touched with flamboyance. But although he was clean and freshly-shaven, there was a different look about him; he gave Gideon the impression of being older. There was a noticeable swelling at his jaw; it had turned a muddy brown in colour with a few purplish marks. Lewisham, his solicitor, was already in court, a man with a mild manner and a turnip-shaped head. He had not yet seen Gideon. The small Press boxes with their wooden seats and wooden upright backs were crowded to overflowing, five men sitting, at least six standing. The slightly larger public gallery was crowded, too; Gideon heard whispering from the constable at the door.

"No more, that's the lot."

He looked at the people in the gallery, wondering if any of them had had anything to do with the robberies or with the murder of Clapper's wife.

There was a hush in the court, as always, and it was almost possible to forget the rush and tear, the ceaseless telephone

calls, the constant to-ing and fro-ing, both outside and at the
office. Yet it wasn't a restful quiet. There was tension here
already, and when the Press saw him there was a sudden
flurry of movement, heads were turned, whispers made the
magistrate, an elderly, silvery-haired man named Bennett,
look towards the box with a frown, and made the magistrate's clerk glare. The glare was almost a trick of the
trade. Lewisham turned round quickly, and saw Gideon;
at the same moment Clapper stared at him. Clapper was
now in the dock, still guarded, and the clerk said waspishly:

"Leonard Clapper, second hearing, remanded for eight
days on a charge of complicity with others unknown in the
robbery at Siddley Bank, Moorgate, on the . . ." He was
brisk and to the point.

The magistrate leaned forward in the ornately carved
arm-chair, which was set against carved oak panels darkened
by the years. He clasped his hands on the dark oak bench in
front of him.

"Are the police ready?" he asked.

Cornish, some distance away from Gideon, said: "Yes,
sir."

"Is the defendant represented?"

Lewisham bobbed up.

"Yes, your honour, and with the court's permission I
would like to make a statement on behalf of the defendant.
The defendant while in custody was the subject of a brutal
assault and —"

"We are not here to try the police, Mr. Lewisham, we are
here to find out whether the police have sufficient evidence
against your client for a committal."

"I do understand, your honour." Lewisham was too
smooth, to obsequious; no one would ever like him, but he
was certainly shrewd – and, thought Gideon, he probably
knew the name of Clapper's accomplices, possibly knew the
murderer of Clapper's wife. "But with the court's permission, your honour, I would like to draw attention to the
painful bruise on my client's face, a very painful bruise
indeed, and in the circumstances I would like to ask your
honour if he will order an independent doctor to examine

my client and to state whether he is fit to plead. In my considered opinion my client has been so badly treated that . . ."

Mr. Bennett heard him out, and then said flatly: "Are you seriously suggesting that the police beat-up your client and that he is not fit to plead?"

"Your Honour, I am only interested in establishing the facts and making sure that my client has the full protection of the law." Mr. Lewisham's voice was softly insistent. He seemed to be saying: "The police have knocked him about, I'm going to make sure that he has a square deal from the court, but from the way you're talking it doesn't seem likely."

"It would only take a short while," he persisted, "and in the interests of justice —"

"I will look after the interests of justice in this court, Mr. Lewisham." Bennett looked at Cornish. "Can the police inform me whether the defendant has been examined by a doctor?"

"Yes, sir, by two doctors. They both —"

"But both are police surgeons —" Lewisham squeaked.

"So the police, the medical profession and the bench are now on trial," said Bennett, caustically. "Have the goodness to let me finish. Superintendent, you were about to tell me what the medical report was, but in the circumstances I think it would be better for us to have one of the doctors present in order to give evidence. Can that be arranged?"

"Yes, sir," Cornish said. "But it may take two or even three hours."

"Then I shall defer this case until three o'clock this afternoon," declared Bennett, glancing at the clock. "I understand from Mr. Miriam that we shall have plenty to keep us occupied until then." He looked down at the clerk.

"We will indeed, sir."

"Thank you, sir," said Cornish. "But I would like permission to make a statement on behalf of the police at this stage."

"Can't it wait, Mr. Cornish?"

"If it does, sir, it will not be reported in the evening newspapers, and the particular circumstances might give rise to some misunderstanding."

"Ah," said Bennett. "Yes. An interesting point." He glanced at Gideon. "You may proceed, Mr. Cornish."

"Thank you sir," said Cornish. "If there were more time I would ask Commander Gideon to —"

"In the interests of justice the court always has plenty of time," said Bennett, and Gideon smothered a grin; the old boy was turning up trumps. "Since this is of such importance would you like to take the oath, Commander?"

"I'd rather leave that until I'm charged with some breach of regulations, sir," Gideon said. "But I would like to state publicly that when I was questioning the defendant I showed him a picture of his wife, taken after death, and that it had such an effect on him that he collapsed, and in collapsing struck his chin heavily on the edge of my desk. I have since had the desk examined by a member of the laboratory staff, sir, and at the appropriate time can show that some fragments of skin, two or three hairs and a trace of blood are at the spot struck by the defendant's chin. His collapse was quite understandable, sir, any man seeing a picture of his wife with her throat slashed like this" – he took a photograph out of his pocket and held it forward – "would surely —"

There was a gasping sound from the dock. Clapper's eyes closed, and he grabbed the rail of the dock as if to save himself from falling. Gideon spared a grateful thought for the police surgeon who had confirmed that one shock reaction to blood or wounds made others likely.

"Thank you, Mr. Gideon, that will do," interrupted the magistrate; "I really cannot have the court used as a public platform any more." Five of the newspapermen were trying to get out at the same moment. "The hearing is adjourned until three o'clock this afernoon. Officers, give the defendant all the attention he needs, and arrange for a doctor . . ."

"Nice work, George," Cornish said, as they met in front of the entrance to the cells. "Anyone would think you laid it all on."

"There's something we can lay on," Gideon said. He

thrust the door open, and saw Clapper, a policewoman, Lewisham and the two constables all in a little group; only Clapper was sitting. He looked up as if in terror when Gideon went in.

"Clapper," Gideon began.

"I must protest —" Lewisham began.

"You shut up," Gideon rasped. "Clapper, why keep it up? Who did this job? You know that whoever did it killed your wife, and all Lewisham's rigmarole won't alter it. You're a liar and he's a liar, that's just been demonstrated."

"Commander . . ."

"Listen, Lewisham," Gideon growled, "you're here by our courtesy. If you want to stay, you keep quiet until I've finished. Clapper —"

"The – the man you want is Scarfe, Alan Scarfe," Clapper muttered in a quavering voice. "He – he also goes under the name of Spender, he's got a flat in Mayling Street leading into Berkeley Square. He was with me at the bank, he —"

"Clapper, stop incriminating yourself!" cried Lewisham.

"All right, Corny, you can get all the rest of the dope," Gideon said, and he looked down at the turnip-shaped head of the lawyer with disgust. "If Lewisham is also Scarfe *alias* Spender's lawyer we might have an interesting side issue. Clapper, if you've got any sense, you'll make a full and complete statement. It's the only sensible thing to do. If the jury has any sympathy for you, you might get yourself a square deal from now on." He didn't wait, but turned to leave the court, knowing that outside there would be a crush of newspapermen and the public. He was right. They called out to him and two men congratulated him, but he simply said without smiling:

"This one isn't our real trouble. The big worry today is the lunatic who started those fires last night – yes, they were all arson. Anyone who gets a whiff of smoke they can't explain ought to ring up the nearest Police Station right away. Remember to tell your editors that, will you?"

He strode to his waiting car.

*　　*　　*

Biship stepped inside the yard of the quarry company's yard at Lambeth, seeing two lorries being loaded with paving stone, and Keen, the manager, directing a mechanical grab. Biship slipped behind some piles of sand and others of rockery stone, and approached Keen's small office.

Biship had been in that office frequently, collecting the weekly payments from men who worked here, and he knew that there were stacks of dynamite in a shed leading from the office. Whenever Keen was away the door was locked, but it would be open now. Of greater importance in some ways were the detonators which Biship would need. Keen kept these in a cupboard behind his desk, and this was usually locked. However, Keen sometimes left his keys in the desk drawer, and Biship knew the cupboard key was a Yale.

He peeped out of the office window, saw Keen still working, turned away and picked up the dynamite without trouble, put the twelve sticks into a leather case, then went to the cupboard.

The door was locked, and Biship was trembling when he pulled out the desk drawer.

The keys were there.

Gideon spent twelve minutes exactly in the canteen for lunch that day, and when he got back to his desk he belched twice, stabbed the bell push and, as the messenger came in, said testily: "Go along to the first aid room and get me some bicarbonate of soda or anything they recommend for indigestion." He turned away from the man as the door closed, and then the telephone bell rang; he felt as if it were growing to his ear "Gideon," he announced, and said a moment later : "Who – *who*?" Bell, who had been to lunch first, looked across in surprise, because it was not often that Gideon sounded taken aback, but this time his expression was startled as well as his voice. "All right, Lem," he said. "Yes, I'll see them." He rang off. "Guess what?" he asked, and then the absurdity of the question occurred to him, and he went on before Bell could answer: "That was Lemaitre. Mr. and Mrs. Ericson have called to see him. And me!"

"Good God!"

"And they had to choose today," Gideon said. "Oh, well. Anything in from Cornish?"

"No," answered Bell. "Not since he called to say that he's going round to the Mayling Street flat that Scarfe rented as Spender. There's a call out for Scarfe – I told you that the description of the man seen with Mrs. Clapper squared with Scarfe's, didn't I?"

"Yes. That old scar should be a help too. But if he was at Mayling Street, I'd have expected Cornish to have picked him up by now," Gideon said. He still felt uneasy about Scarfe *alias* Spender although he did not say so. He kept picturing Mrs. Clapper's throat wound, and telling himself that a man who could do that could do anything. Before, when Cornish had been longer than expected without reporting, Gideon had felt uneasy. He told himself that there was no need this time; and in any case, Cornish wouldn't go alone to see a killer.

Gideon's telephone bell rang, and the door opened at a tap. He caught a glimpse of a woman and Lemaitre, with a man behind them. The woman was tall and nicely turned out; Gideon first noticed her slender body and almost too slim legs; she was beautifully dressed in something rather bottle green in colour, and she wore a mink stole. Ericson, who followed her in as Lemaitre stood rather awkwardly on one side, had a military air about him; he looked pale; the woman quite composed.

Gideon said: "Take a seat, Mrs. Ericson, won't keep you a jiff." Into the telephone, he announced: "Gideon." His whole expression changed when he went on: "Are you sure?" and it must have been obvious to the woman and the man as well as to Lemaitre and Bell that he had forgotten them, forgotten everything but what the man was saying. "Thank God for that. Have the street watched, make sure that he can't be scared off. He's probably got eyes like a hawk. Okay, Lucky!" He rang off, and said to Bell: "Margetson says they've found where Biship is living – calls himself Brown, and has digs in a house in Blackheath." He could not keep the light out of his eyes when he looked up at Mrs. Ericson, who was sitting with her shoulders square,

very upright in an arm-chair. Her husband was sitting on
an upright chair. Lemaitre, intense and earnest until that
moment, was shaken by the news from Gideon, and asked:

"Haven't picked him up though, have they?"

"They will," said Gideon. "Well, what can I do for you?"
He glanced at Ericson, knowing already that he was in a
highly nervous state; the woman probably was, too, but she
had a quality it was hard to define unless it was born of self-
confidence and breeding. She might have stepped out of an
advertisement in *Woman's Home Journal*, she was so
polished and correct.

There was a tap at the door, and the messenger entered,
carrying a medicine glass with liquid in it. Gideon almost
gaped. Bell made a noise in his throat. Then Gideon said:
"Thanks," took the glass, threw his head back, and tipped
the bicarbonate of soda down.

"Got a cold coming on," he said, casually. "Now, will you
please —"

"Mrs. Ericson says —" Lemaitre interrupted. He caught
Gideon's eye and stopped in mid-sentence.

"It is very good of you to see us, especially on a day when
you must be so very busy." Mrs. Ericson took her oppor-
unity swiftly and easily. "I am here with my husband
because I am really responsible for what has happened."
That came out so smoothly. "It concerned the issue of New
Rand Iron Ore Company, of course – your Department has
been making inquiries about the issue of fifty thousand one-
pound shares at par."

"Mr. Lemaitre has reported to me in detail," Gideon said,
and he looked at the man, not at the woman. "I understand
there is some doubt as to the accuracy of the surveyor's
reports."

"It wasn't until Mr. Lemaitre began to make inquiries
that we realised what might have happened," Mrs. Ericson
declared, and already it seemed obvious to Gideon then that
the Ericsons were going to turn on Roscoe. Had there been
an arrangement? Was Roscoe going to take the rap for a
pay-off later? That was the kind of theory that Lemaitre
would advance but he himself shouldn't, thought Gideon as

Mrs. Ericson went on: "The absurd thing is that it is really my fault, Mr. Gideon."

"Oh." Gideon felt deflated.

"Yes," said Mrs. Ericson, calmly. "I misread the report which came in from Mr. Roscoe while he was in Africa. I'm afraid it is a question of a little knowledge being a dangerous thing. I studied it, misread the percentage of ore content, and made copies of it together with my recommendations. That was used in all negotiations, because I lost the original report."

Gideon thought: Oh, did you, sceptically.

"All of us were careless, Mr. Gideon," Mrs. Ericson went on, "but I can only hope that we weren't criminally careless. The assumptions we made from the report were wrong. We issued the shares in good faith, but it might well look as if we were attempting to defraud the public. We are here to assure you that nothing of the kind was in our mind. In fact —" She broke off, and glanced up, as if she wanted her husband to say something; and Ericson took his cue, for he followed on almost as if he were repeating a carefully learned lesson:

"In fact we are desperately distressed by it, because of the reputation of our firm – it was established nearly seventy years ago," he declared, his voice very husky. "My grandfather started it, and my father inherited it from him. I came into it with rather too little training, I'm afraid."

Lemaitre's look was saying: "I don't believe a word of this, don't be fooled, George," and Gideon wondered what was coming next. He was in a strangely brittle mood, and anxious at the same time; he wanted word from Cornish, and prayed for news that Biship had been held. There was still a possibility that Biship wasn't the man they wanted, but he did not think it likely.

". . . what we propose to do," said Mrs. Ericson, still the main spokesman, "is to offer to buy back at par. We have already made provisional arrangements. One difficulty, as my husband had pointed out, is that some of the smaller shareholders especially will suspect that we might be wanting to buy back because we think the shares are already increasing in value. It's almost as if we will be misunderstood whichever way we act, isn't it?"

Gideon's thoughts were wrenched off Biship.

"Caught between two stools," he said, ponderously. "Yes, I see what you mean. Well, Mr. Ericson, what kind of reputation you have as a firm is hardly our concern. Our concern is simply to make sure that the law isn't broken, and if it is broken, to investigate all the circumstances and to make a charge whenever those circumstances appear to justify it. I can tell you that doubts about the regularity of this share issue have been raised, and papers are being studied here and in the Public Prosecutor's Office, but no action has yet been recommended. At the moment you say you are ready to buy these shares back. Such an action could influence the kind of charge made, if any. Certainly no harm could come from it."

The woman's eyes were narrow and watchful.

Ericson said: "But you could still prefer a charge —"

"Mr. Ericson, I hope you'll understand me if I say that I think you might be more wisely represented by your solicitor," said Gideon. "I'm sure he will agree that your contemplated action would be in everyone's best interests, and my knowledge of the Public Prosecutor's Office is that they never make a charge unless they are positive of criminal intent." That was as far as he dare go, perhaps further than he should. "Now if you will excuse me, I've another very urgent appointment. These fires that are worrying us." He hoisted his huge frame out of his chair, and towered over Ericson; to the obvious surprise of both husband and wife, he offered his hand. The woman seemed much less tense than she had been, and the gleam in Ericson's eyes suggested that he felt that a crisis had been passed.

They went out, Lemaitre opening the door for them, and behind their backs, Lemaitre frowned at Gideon, as if to ask: "What's going on?"

Bell's telephone rang, and Bell lifted the receiver instantly.

"Bell speaking . . . Eh? . . . Hold on a minute." He looked across at Gideon, and there was the too familiar tautness in his voice; tension was in everyone today. This concerned Biship, of course – and drove all thought of the Ericsons away. "Biship was last seen in Blackheath by one of his customers from a round he does there," Bell went on. "He was by himself, and on foot. No doubt about the identification."

"Blackheath," echoed Gideon, and stared at the map. "Better buzz ST and QR. Have all roads watched for pedestrians and cyclists carrying packages, check all buses, all Green Line services, all cars."

"You'll have Traffic on your back, George."

"Better than having London burning about my ears," Gideon growled. "But I ought to have a word with them. Ta." He called the Commander of the Traffic Department of the Metropolitan Police, explained what he wanted to do, and put it in such a way that he seemed to be asking for permission.

"Oh, you hold up all London's traffic," the other Commander said sarcastically. "Then see what happens if you don't pick up your chap by the rush hour. You haven't got long."

"We won't cause any more disturbance than we must," said Gideon. "Lay it on with your chaps, will you?"

"Do your job for you now," grumbled the other. "All right, George." Gideon said thanks and replaced the receiver. Bell grinned across, and they had a few minutes of quiet, without even a telephone call. Bell made notes, and Gideon sat back and tried to think of anything they had missed in the hunt for Biship. The fact that Cornish hadn't yet reported began to nag, too, and Mrs. Ericson's story began to stir in his mind, too.

Suddenly the door was pushed open and Lemaitre came in, saying: "Talk about one law for the rich and one for the poor, but I daresay you've been right, George. That was the last thing I expected, and even if she lied like a trooper, you can bet your life she'd go down tops with the jury. We'd never make a case stick." Before Gideon had time to comment, a telephone rang on Gideon's desk, and Bedlam was back. Gideon picked up the receiver, said: "Hold on a minute," and looked up at Lemaitre. "We'll see, Lem. Nip out to Hoppy's place, will you, and among other things have a talk with Tiny Repp. Hoppy's been holding him for looting."

"Who, Tiny? Hoppy gone mad?"

"He thinks Tiny fell to temptation," said Gideon, who knew that Lemaitre had a soft spot for the big burglar. "Could be right, too, but Tiny swears he thought he was being a hero. Don't let Hoppy know that's what you're after. Tell him you're making a tour of the Divisions to keep everything keyed up for Biship."

"Okay," said Lemaitre, "and I'll tell you what I think about the Ericsons another time. Anything in from Cornish?"

"No," Gideon answered.

Lemaitre went out, still deflated, and there was another spell of silence before two telephones rang at once, one on each desk. The two men lifted their receivers with simultaneous movements, and spoke together. "Gideon." "Bell." Gideon observed all this, and smiled wryly to himself as he heard a man say in a hurried voice: "Smith of Information here, sir. There's a man on the line who says he's seen Biship today, says that Biship's gone off with a dozen sticks of TNT. I'm holding him on. He's speaking from a quarrying firm in Lambeth."

It was like being struck by a blast of hot air.

"Send men there, to stay with this chap. I'll go and see him," Gideon said, and began to stand up while he was talking. Horror seemed to close about him as the full significance of this news struck him. "Have a driver at my car, with the name and address of this quarrying company, in three minutes." He banged the receiver down and rounded the desk. "Biship's loose with enough stuff on him to blow up whole districts," he declared. "Keep in touch with me on the radio." He went striding out of the office, at his most aggressive, and he did not believe that he had ever been more worried.

As he neared a corner, Lemaitre came hurrying round it, his face split in two with a grin.

"Hey, George, I've just realised what you put me on to Tiny Repp for. I've got to lay off the Ericsons, but when it comes to —"

Lemaitre broke off, at Gideon's expression.

"We're in trouble, Biship's got hold of some dynamite," Gideon said. "See Bell and tell him to alert Carmichael, this could start any time." He went striding on, with Lemaitre staring after him.

CHAPTER XVII

MADMAN'S FOLLY

THE man, Keen, had very bright blue eyes, narrowed just now, thin lips and a rock-like face; he wasn't a man to take to. He stood in his office at the big yard, dwarfed by Gideon, surrounded by great piles of crazy paving, rockery stone and wall stone. He wore a check lumber jacket of grey and white, he was unshaven, and trying to put a bold face on the situation.

"I've already told your chaps twice," he said resentfully to Gideon. "I thought Biship came here to collect his dough – he missed last week. It wasn't until I saw a newspaper with his photograph on that I tied him up with the fires." Keen motioned to the dynamite store visible through the open doorway. "Then I checked that stuff, and I didn't lose a sec. calling you chaps. I didn't dream —"

"All right," Gideon said. "It was a hell of a thing to happen, but no one's blaming you. How powerful were these sticks?"

"Each one could blow up a house," Keen told him, and moistened his lips.

"What time was Biship here?"

"I've already told —"

"Tell me."

"It must have been just after twelve," Keen said. "I was

surprised, because he doesn't usually come on Thursdays, his regular calling day is Monday. He was going out when I saw him. I was on a rush job, and I told myself if he couldn't wait I wasn't in any hurry to pay him.

"Turned right out of the gates towards Shooters Hill, that's all I can tell you."

That would tally with the report already in.

"All right, Mr. Keen, thanks," he said, and turned round to his driver. "Pierce, get the Assistant Commissioner on the radio for me, I'll be at the car as soon as you've got him." The driver hurried out. When Gideon followed, the driver was holding out the microphone, and Gideon took it and slid into his seat. "Hallo, A.C." That was as familiar as he allowed himself to get when subordinates were present. "Biship's running round loose with a dozen sticks of TNT. I've alerted Carmichael, Bell's busy on it, Traffic's co-operating, but I don't know whether we ought to use the radio and television to step up the search. Wouldn't warn the people what he's got, would you?"

"I'll talk to the Commissioner," Rogerson, the A.C., said. "Bell tells me you might have Biship surrounded."

"Might's the operative word," Gideon growled. "I'm going to see Rickett at ST, and I'll keep to the main roads."

"Right," said Rogerson.

Gideon nodded to the driver, who was already starting the engine. The headquarters of ST Division was less than a mile away, and Gideon knew that he was going to see the man simply because he could no longer sit and wait in the office. He kept the radio on as reports flashed to and fro, and practically every one had to do with Biship. One man who had gone mad could do this. One man —

He heard a man say clearly: "There's been an explosion in Market Street, Whitechapel. Get all roads approaching Market Street cleared of traffic."

Gideon closed his eyes; it was as if a great weight was pressing down upon him.

Walter Biship was astride a motor-scooter, one which he had bought second-hand that morning. On some of his rounds he had preferred a motor-scooter to a car, because it was easier to handle. He was thoroughly familiar with the little machine. His knowledge of the East End – in fact most of London south of the river from Battersea to Woolwich – was invaluable, too. He knew the short cuts. He knew the places where a fire was likely to take hold quickest. He knew that on a small machine like this he could dart about the traffic on the main roads, and make it almost impossible for anyone to catch him. He had chosen a route carefully, using a pencil and paper to trace a map of London, then making pencilled notes of those places where he proposed to start the fires.

The oil and paint warehouse in Wapping was the first obvious place. It was in the middle of a vast built-up area, with a web of narrow streets, many of them children's playgrounds, a few big blocks of tenements, warehouses filled to overflowing with inflammable goods, timber yards, petrol stations, and a paper warehouse. He knew that if he could once get a big fire started there, it would bring the major fire services from all the neighbouring districts. He had seen exactly how this concentration had been effected the night before; by day it would not be so easy, because of the traffic on the road. Fire-engines would be later reaching the danger spots, and the risk of the fire gaining a firm hold was much greater. He also knew that it would have to be a widespread series of outbreaks; one isolated fire, even a big one, would be comparatively easy to control. That was why he had planned his route carefully, while sitting at Mrs. Tennison's.

It would take him only ten or twelve minutes to ride round, and to hurl a stick of TNT fitted with a detonator which would go off on contact, at seven different places on the perimeter of a kind of circle. He selected the paint warehouse first because he could throw it over the back wall with little fear of being seen. The next spot on the route was a waste paper and rag merchant where big stocks of rags, many of them thick and dirty with oil, were stored. He could drive past the open gates of this place and toss a second stick of TNT in. Beyond that was a timber yard, next on the route a petrol station which backed on to a big

warehouse filled with children's toys and in turn flanked by
general warehouses. The fourth place was another, smaller
paint store, chosen because it was in the right position. Fifth
and sixth were general warehouses, one filled mostly with
cigarettes and one with cotton goods. The seventh place was
the main works and head offices of a dry cleaning plant,
where the cleaning fluids would go up in a flash.

Now that he had marked out his map carefully, Biship
felt surprisingly cool, and also felt a deep, satisfying sense
of accomplishment. He would achieve something really
worthwhile now. He would not only avenge the death of his
wife and daughter, but would have destroyed those hated
parts of London where he had lived and worked all his life.
It would be The Third Fire of London.

He turned the corner of the narrow street near the first
of his objectives, and saw two cyclists further along, coming
towards him; no one else was in the street. He slowed down
until the cyclists had passed, then put on a spurt. As he
passed the high wall of the paint warehouse, he tossed the
stick of dynamite. He put on a spurt, and was fifty yards
away before the explosion came. He swung round the corner
towards the Mile End Road – and there, standing shocked
by the deafening roar of the explosion, were two uniformed
policemen.

They were so shaken that they did not seem to notice him,
and the scooter roared past. He made one mistake – looking
over his shoulder to see if they were taking any notice of
him. Both had turned round. By then doors were opening,
windows were being flung up, here and there glass was
starred by the blast. There were more explosions as tins or
paint exploded under the sudden heat of the fire. Biship
swung round another corner, then another, feeling sure that
he had shaken the two men off. In any case, they had been
on foot, they hadn't a chance to catch him – and the next
objective was only three minutes' ride away.

He turned towards it, and as he did so, a police car came
hurtling along the road towards him, a man beside the
driver waving him down. At the same moment, a fire-engine

swung into sight. As he was forced to slow down, the driver shouted at him:

"Keep off the road until you're told you can move."

Biship pulled into the kerb, sat astride his little machine for a few seconds, and then climbed off it. His mind was as alert as it had ever been, and he realised that these policemen didn't suspect him, yet. But they would soon catch up with the men who had seen him coming round the corner, so he had only a few minutes of safety. He began to walk rapidly away from his machine, glancing behind him every now and again. Already there was a great plume of smoke in the sky, he had started off perfectly. *The Third Fire of London!* He turned a corner and went into a street where a big crowd had gathered, held back at a road junction so that fire-engines could get past. There were excited people and worried people, there were frightened people and bold ones.

The police took no notice of the little man who pushed past the cordon out of the road where the traffic was stopped, except one middle-aged policeman named Edwards, from the NE Division. He caught a glimpse of Biship out of the corner of his eye, and was then pushed in the back by half a dozen youths who wanted to get nearer. He kept them at bay, and raised his voice so that it sounded even above the roar of the fire-engines. The Fire Service, standing by for just such an emergency, was going into action like an army.

"Sergeant!" Edwards bellowed, and a sergeant saw him and heard him and stalked to him. *"Think I saw Biship!"* Edwards gasped. "Going down there, wearing a grey raincoat and a triby!"

"Okay," the sergeant said, and ran towards a police car which had a radio.

Gideon picked up the message as he was swinging towards the NE Division, having countermanded his orders to go to NZ. As soon as it came in, he ordered:

"Seal off the whole of the area within a mile radius of the spot where Biship was seen. Yes, I know it might be a false alarm, but do it." He heard the, "Yes, sir," and then was told: "The Assistant Commissioner would like a word with you, sir."

"Right," said Gideon.

"George," said the A.C., almost at once, "radio and television programmes are being interrupted to warn people in the East and Central London areas. Information Room is concentrating on this job except for one team. Biship was seen on the motor-scooter at . . ." Rogerson named a place half a mile from the paint warehouse – and then at the warehouse at Billton Street. Got your map?"

"Yes," Gideon said. "That means he's travelling east from the first point, and there's the big Willison warehouse block there so he's probably been forced to go slightly south-east."

"I'll see it's all covered," the A.C. promised. "Where are you going now?"

"The first fire," said Gideon, and then realised that he had said 'first' although so far there was only one. "Another thing, we told all factories which were vulnerable to arrange a special guard, and now we'd better send a message to all places within the area of NE and QR Divisions. Better take men off the door-to-door job quick, and send them in detachments to petrol stations, gas-works, petrol depots, warehouses, waste and cotton warehouses, timber yards —"

"I'll see to it," the Assistant Commissioner promised.

Gideon sat back. His driver, slowed down at a traffic light, glanced at him curiously, and saw the perspiration on his forehead, the thrust of his big jaw. Gideon placed the map on his knees, drew a half circle round the spots where he thought there was likely to be trouble, and muttered: "The truth is he means to start a big 'un. If he's worked it out properly he'll make a circle of fires." He stabbed at the map with a ball point pen, and called out the names of streets and places to his driver. He had never acted with fiercer speed or greater decision, and he had never been so frightened.

Biship was frightened, too

He had not reckoned on such an immediate mobilisation of the police and the Fire Service. Wherever he went there were signs of them, and on foot he had no time to get round. He turned a corner some minutes' walk from his second objective, the waste merchant's, and saw a bicycle leaning against the wall. It was a small machine, probably a child's, but he was a small man. He hurried up, pushed it and jumped astride. He heard someone call out, but pedalled furiously along the street, turned a corner, and saw the entrance to the warehouse – and two policemen getting off bicycles in front of it.

He had the stick of TNT in his hand.

One of the policemen saw it, and gave a deep bull-like roar. Biship flung the stick, high in the air. One of the policemen ducked and covered his head and shoulders, the other one leapt at Biship. Biship passed within a foot of him, kicking out with his right leg. He cracked his shoe into the man's face as the policeman tried to grab the moving bicycle, and heard the sound; a moment later the explosion came. He went on furiously, swung round a corner, and saw more policemen and plainclothes men strung along the road, obviously hurrying to some rendezvous. It was like a peep-show. One moment, they were all walking away from Biship, then the roar of the explosion came, and every man stopped, every head jerked round.

Biship had another stick in his hand, and the glitter in his eye was so vicious that it looked as if he would throw it along the line of men. Instead, he swung his wheel in the opposite direction.

Men began to run after him.

He turned the next corner, where a solitary policeman was hurrying along the middle of the road. It was one with empty houses on either side, some of them already under the demolition machines. A hundred yards away was a public house, and on the opposite corner a general shop. Biship's next objective was half a mile away, and he knew of a short cut – but the policeman stood between him and that narrow lane.

The policeman's name was Lee. He was twenty-three. He had been in the Force for eighteen months, and only seven months on his own beat. He always followed every move and every order, every request and every teleprint message as closely as a student studied his books, and he had studied Biship's photograph just as closely. He had just been told that Biship was going round with sticks of TNT in his pocket, blowing places up.

He saw Biship riding furiously towards him on the bicycle. He saw the glitter and the glare in the man's eyes. He stood quite still. In a strange way it was like being on the Rugby field, waiting for the other man to swerve. Biship came very close, and P.C. Lee did not move. Suddenly, Biship swerved to the left. Lee saw what he was going to do, and leapt at him. He caught Bishop round the waist, and they crashed down – and before Lee even realised that he was hurt, all the remaining sticks of dynamite blew up.

Two policemen, chasing after Biship, saw the whole incident from the corner. One flung himself down in time to miss the worst of the explosion; the other was badly injured in the head and chest.

Gideon was half a mile away when the news came through. At first, he could hardly believe that it was true, but the reports were emphatic, and when he heard details of the sacrifice of P.C. Lee he had no further doubts. His driver looked at him, and saw that he was moistening his lips.

He said: "Looks as if that's over. Take me on to NE headquarters, will you?" He sat back, staring straight ahead of him, hearing the reports going to and fro through the air, noting the relief and the jubilation in the voices of men as the one phrase was repeated over and over again:

"We've got him."

Five minutes later, the car pulled up outside the old Victorian building which houses NE Division – a fire-trap, if ever there was one. Hopkinson, tall, thin, with a well-brushed and recently showered air, was standing in the hall with Lemaitre, who was smiling. Gideon went in. The charge room was on the right, and someone was talking in there, indignantly. Gideon ignored the talk, but said to Hopkinson:

"If you can't find me a quick one, I'll have your stripes."

"Come up to the office," Hopkinson said. He looked shocked. "You look as if you can do with one, George. Heard how it ended? One of my chaps did it, chap named Lee. Wouldn't have thought he had the guts, he was always throwing the book about."

"Married?"

"No. Only son," said Hopkinson. "It's a hell of a business. I —"

"Mr. Gideon!" a man shouted, from behind Gideon, and he looked over his shoulder to see an enormous creature, who towered even over him, striding after him, big face aflame with indignation, thick lips parted, great hands outstretched. "Mr. Gideon, I swear to you on my mother's dying body, I never went to do no looting. I thought old Gran Muggs was up in that bedroom, deaf as a post Gran is, and as Gawd's my judge, I went to get her out. I've run straight for over two years, Mr. Gideon, I've got a decent job, I'd be crazy to throw all that away. Can't you make Mr. Hopkinson and Old Lem see sense?"

There was a pause.

Hopkinson said: "All right, Tiny, we'll take your word for it this time."

The delight on the big man's face was remarkable to see.

It was a little after six o'clock when Gideon entered his office again. Bell was still there, relaxing with his feet up on the desk, pipe going, a cup of tea or coffee at his elbow. He moved his feet as Gideon went in, and said:

"Why didn't you go straight home, George? The Yard won't fall down if you're not here every minute."

"I need it more than it needs me, known that for a long time," said Gideon. "I'm on my way home, anyhow. Seen all the reports?"

"Yes."

"Much damage?"

"Only one big fire, and that's under control. Not much doubt that he was going to ring the whole area, George. Five deaths, one in the explosion at the first place, one our man Lee. Wonder how many chaps like Lee we've got."

"Plenty," said Gideon, gruffly. He sat on the corner of his desk, smoothed the surface of his pipe inside his pocket, and said : "I've just seen his mother. She looked – oh well, you know. We've got to get a posthumous George Medal for Lee, Joe." He paused. "Anything in from Cornish?"

"No."

"Couldn't have run into trouble, could he?"

"Shouldn't think he would worry to report unless he had some good news," Bell said, comfortably. "We've had Riddell on the line, though. He's going to hold Harrison in the morning. Looks cast iron."

"Well, he stuck to it and he's fixed it," Gideon said, and then the door opened, and a tired but relaxed Margetson came in.

"Just come from the place where Biship was living," he said promptly. "He has an old Olivetti, and there were some sketch maps of the area he was in today. His landlady said she couldn't believe it, he was such a nice man. The more I see of the reports, the more it's obvious that when his wife and daughter were burned to death it turned his mind. Never was a hundred per cent normal, I should think." Margetson rubbed his eyes. "Got to admit I'm tired now, George."

"You go and get some sleep," said Gideon. "Seen Carmichael?"

"He was busy at the big fire, but was going home when I left. He said he'd call you in the morning."

"Right," said Gideon, and Margetson went to the door. There was a chorus of good nights, and the door closed. Gideon stared out of the window at the brightness of the Thames, heard the roar of the late home-going traffic, and said: "I wish Cornish would come through." He stifled a yawn. "I'll go and see Priddy, and make sure —"

He broke off, when the door opened, and Cornish came in. It was impossible to judge anything from his expression except that he wasn't jubilant. Gideon felt a wave of relief, and realised how much he had worried about a repeat performance by Mrs. Clapper's killer.

"Hallo, George," Cornish said. "Had quite a time, haven't you?"

"I survived," Gideon said. "Going to be a mess to clear up, and I wouldn't mind betting that every newspaper leader tomorrow says that it's past time something was done to clear the slums we've still got." He broke off. "Any luck?"

"No," answered Cornish, heavily. "Not since Clapper gave us Spender's name and address. Spender hasn't been at Mayling Street for three days and nights. It's pretty clear that he kept one set of clothes there, one set of everything he needed, but it wasn't much more than a *pied-à-terre*. I wouldn't mind betting that he's known for some time that he couldn't be too sure of the Clappers, and he's made himself a third identity somewhere. Might be halfway across the world for all we know."

Gideon grunted: "Pity. But we'll get him."

In fact, Scarfe *alias* Spender *alias* Simpson was not half-way across the world, but he was halfway across the Channel in an aircraft. His passport was under the name of Simpson, and he did not think there would be any trouble at the other side. Whether he would ever be able to return to England safely was a different matter, and deep down in him there was a fear that one day he might be identified, one day there might be an extradition order for him. But for the time being, he was safe.

Gideon opened the front door of his home, heard the piano being played with a touch which only Penelope had, walked past the front room, and saw Kate sitting in front of the television in the living-room; a conjuror was doing remarkable things with a white handkerchief. Kate looked round, leaned forward immediately and switched off, and said:

"George, you look tired out."

"I'm all right," Gideon said. "Nothing a good night's sleep won't cure." He stood in front of her, held her arms firmly, and looked straight into her clear grey eyes. "How about Helen today. She all right?"

"I told you last night that there wasn't anything to worry about," Kate said. "Two days in bed, and she'll be as right as I am."

"So she was wrong about a baby," Gideon said.

"I'm not sure, and I don't suppose I ever will be," Kate said quietly. "I have a feeling that Jane Miall was more determined than anyone to make sure that if they marry, it won't be under compulsion, and I have an idea —"

Gideon put his hand on Kate's knee.

"Forget it, Kate."

"I suppose I must," Kate said, with a smile, but her expression was serious as she went on: "Ted Miall still thinks in terms of marriage as an obligation. With the baby, I think I would too, but now I don't know what to say."

"I know this," said Gideon. "Matthew and Helen will do what they want, whatever we or Ted Miall says, and I for one am damned glad they won't let themselves be panicked into marriage. It wouldn't surprise me if they changed their tune in a few months' time, but now – if Ted Miall's got any sense, he won't drive Helen too far, or he'll drive her away from home."

"I think you can leave Ted to his wife," Kate said, mildly.

"She can handle him just as well as you can handle me," Gideon remarked dryly. After a pause, he went on: "Anything in the oven? I'm as hungry as a horse."

"I'll get your nosebag," Kate said, and squeezed his hand, then stood up.

"I'll get you a drink, that and a tablet will give you the best night you've had in years," Harrison said to his wife. "You get into bed and I'll bring it up to you. Okay?"

"Thank you everso, Tony," Pamela said, and her eyes lit up.

Harrison went hurrying down the stairs, and she heard him whistling. It was a long time since she had felt that he was really happy, a long time since she had felt he cared about her at all. She lay on her pillows, looking at her reflection in the dressing-table mirror, seeing two pots of

expensive make-up. When Tony returned, carrying two
glasses which seemed to contain the same brown liquid,
there were tears in her eyes.

She took the glass he handed to her.

"Here's to a good night's sleep," he said, and chinked his
glass against hers.

She didn't like the strong, bitter flavour, but it didn't
worry her, and Tony drank his drink just as quickly.

Ten minutes later, she was asleep.

When Superintendent Riddell reached the Brighton
Police Headquarters next morning, a little before nine
o'clock, he was all set to make the arrest. He went upstairs
to an office which he shared with a local man, and went in.

The Brighton superintendent, an elderly officer, looked up
and said:

"Queer turn-up with Harrison, Rid. His wife's been
found dead – died of an overdose of sleeping tablets. That's
the doctor's first opinion anyhow. Harrison himself was out
all night, at Chloe Duval's place. He went home about
eight this morning to get some clothes, and found the body."

The Brighton man broke off and stared at Riddell, who
had lost all his colour, and whose eyes held a look of horror.

"All right, Rid, come up as soon as you can," Gideon
said. "And don't start kicking yourself. There was no
reason at all to think Harrison's wife was next on the list . . .
We can't do anything about her, but we can get Harrison
for the earlier jobs even if we can't pin this on to him. You
take it easy."

He rang off, but kept a hand on the receiver for several
seconds, while he stared out of the window, the plane trees
and the sky. He could so easily have encouraged Riddell to
pick up Harrison yesterday, and then this might not have
happened. Was there no end to the mistakes a man could
make, unwittingly? Must he be damned to blindness such
as this?

If Harrison had killed his wife, as Riddell obviously
believed, that was one thing. If she'd committed suicide

then neither he nor Riddell need have any regrets. There was no need to assume the worst.

No man could have second sight, anyhow.

The telephone rang beneath his hand, and he picked up the receiver.

THE END

Also by John Creasey
Writing as J. J. Marric

GIDEON'S RISK

"Borgman's too big. He's got too many influential
friends and far too much money. He's the cat's
whiskers, and don't you forget it."
Gideon had been warned, but he knew that the
millionaire had killed his wife over four years ago to
inherit her money, and is determined to prove that
the law for both rich and poor is the same. This is the
measure of the man; that he is prepared to take on
Borgman in the midst of all his other more squalid
preoccupations – all the sex crimes, the petty thefts,
the dopings, the murders – that go to make London's
crime what it is.
"A portrait emerges that is probably very much like
that of a good police officer, the portrait of a man
both tough and conscientious, not intellectual, but
extremely shrewd. Mr. Marric is blazing a significant
trail." Julian Symons in **The Sunday Times**

OTHER GIDEON BOOKS IN CORONET